T·H·E B·A·S·Q·U·E H·O·T·E·L

THE BASQUE SERIES

BOOKS BY ROBERT LAXALT

Violent Land: Tales the Old Timers Tell

Sweet Promised Land

A Man in the Wheatfield

Nevada

In A Hundred Graves: A Basque Portrait

Nevada: A History

A Cup of Tea in Pamplona

The Basque Hotel

A Time We Knew
Images of Yesterday in the Basque Homeland
with photos by William Albert Allard

Child of the Holy Ghost

The

R·O·B·E·R·T   L·A·X·A·L·T

Basque

UNIVERSITY OF NEVADA PRESS RENO & LAS VEGAS

Hotel

Basque Series Editor: William A. Douglass

The paper used in this book meets the minimum requirements of American
National Standard for Information Sciences—ANSI Z39.48-1984. Binding
materials were selected for strength and durability.

University of Nevada Press, Reno, Nevada 89557 USA
Copyright © 1989 Robert Laxalt.
All rights reserved
Designed by Richard Hendel
Printed in the United States of America

9 8 7 6 5 4 3 2 1

Library of Congress Cataloging-in-Publication Data
Laxalt, Robert, 1923–
The Basque Hotel / Robert Laxalt.
p.   cm. — (The Basque series)
ISBN 0-87417-145-8
ISBN 0-87417-216-0 (pbk: alk. paper)
I. Title.   II. Series.
PS3562.A9525B3   1989
813'.54—dc 20   89-4953
CIP

for Grace Bordewich

P · A · R · T   O · N · E

S · U · M · M · E · R

1

Along the length of Main Street, the business people of Carson City had come out to sweep the sidewalks in front of their shops and stores and little hotels. They did this when the sun had barely cleared the desert mountains to the east with a blinding burst of light, and before it had time to bake the sidewalks to a furnace heat.

The boy Pete had made the mistake of waking up before his brothers and sisters, and so his mother had thrust a broom into his hands. His father was usually the one who did the sweeping, but he had been gone all the night before on a mysterious errand. It was his coming home in the darkness before dawn that roused the boy, and he had gone outside in time to see the eastern horizon lined with an irregular band of red. To the west where the forested mountains reared, the sky was purple, so that the dying moon with one star at its tip still shone brilliantly white.

Pete told himself he had made a mistake in waking too early. But the truth was that he liked the sweeping and loved the morning. He liked particularly to sweep the cracks in the sidewalk, turning the broom on edge to clear the dust that had lodged there from the day before. He swept the cigar butts and the rare cigarette butts that the dandies smoked into the gutter, too, but only to make it worthwhile for the street cleaner who would come by later with his push broom and oversized dust pan and the metal trash can he pushed along on wheels.

The boy was lulled by the stillness of the early morning. Whenever he paused in his sweeping, there was no sound to be heard for minutes at a time. He did not count the crow of a late-waking cock from the edge of town or the chirping of birds in the cottonwoods and poplars that covered the back streets and the big white frame houses like a canopy. Those were sounds that were always there, so he did not even hear them.

A block away down the street, he saw the first squaws in their hooded blankets shuffle into sight and sit down on the sidewalk against the buildings to warm their old bones in the beginning sunlight. A block further on, he heard Frank the barber say good morning to one of the politicians who had come for his daily shave. Out of the corner of his eye, the boy saw a movement above him in one of the two windows that flanked the faded black lettering that said "The Basque Hotel," and he knew that Tristant the sheepherder was up and about. Then he heard the cough and sputter of an automobile being cranked to a start somewhere far down the street.

He began to sweep furiously to finish the sidewalk, taking care to go one width of a broom over the property line to the Columbo Hotel next door, because his father had told him that this was good manners to a neighbor. Piumbo, the fat proprietor of the Columbo, came outside just then with a broom. He was smoking a vile cigar that fouled the morning air, and his eyes were puffy and shot with red. The boy guessed this was from drinking too much wine, because he had heard snatches of Piumbo's singing far into the night. Piumbo acknowledged the gesture of the sweeping with a burst of mixed Italian and English, none of which the boy understood.

The time of stillness was gone, and the day had begun.

2

Pete was never sure whether Tristant the Basque sheepherder
liked him or not. It seemed to depend upon what time of day
Tristant saw the boy. This morning was one of those times when
Tristant did not like him. Pete understood why. The household
was still asleep—except of course for his mother, who always seemed
to be awake. Tristant was sitting alone at the long table that ran the
length of the dining room. The box of Kellogg's Corn Flakes was planted
squarely in front of his place, and he was shoveling cereal and milk into
his mouth as fast as he could. When Pete sat down, Tristant glanced at
him venomously and moved the box even closer to his bowl.

Pete could have started the day out well for Tristant if he had chosen
to. He knew and Tristant knew that the box of corn flakes was the only
one left in the hotel. Tristant's craving exceeded his own, because as
his father had told him, cereal and milk were something sheepherders
could not get in the hills.

Pete had already decided he did not want corn flakes this morning,
but coffee and milk with bread soaked in it instead. He also decided
to indulge the mean streak his mother said he possessed. From under
the fringes of his uncombed shock of brown hair, he peered around
the table as though making up his mind what he was going to have for
breakfast. From time to time, he glanced covertly at the box of corn
flakes. Tristant began to eat so fast he was dribbling milk from the corners of his mouth. When he emptied his bowl, he heaped it full again
with so much cereal that it was overflowing. Then he shook the box
and panic came into his eyes, because there was still some left.

Pete did not consider himself as mean as his mother made him out to
be. There was a point at which he relented a little. He did so now with
a sigh as of deep sacrifice, and glumly filled his bowl with coffee and
milk and bread crusts and then poured a mound of sugar over it all.
Tristant stole a guilty look at the boy and slowed the pace of his eating
long enough to give him a smile that showed the gold teeth of which
he was so proud. He mumbled good morning in Basque and the boy
answered him in English.

3

After breakfast Pete went to the kitchen, but he did not stay long. It was uncomfortably hot from the fire in the massive black cooking range fed by firewood and would get more so through the day. Absently, he watched his mother chop vegetables on the cutting block with sure strokes of a big knife and drop them into the soup for the boarders' evening meal. Her forehead was beaded with sweat and her face was strained. Something was on her mind and she was in no mood for talking. Pete picked some flies off the hanging flypaper and went out into the back yard to feed MacTavish.

Shadowed by the big wooden hulk of the Columbo Hotel next door, the back yard was cool and quiet. The black earth had not begun to heat up yet, and next to the fence, it still held the night's dew. The boy felt peace wash over him again and he knew a twinge of remorse for having tormented poor Tristant, who was so ignorant he could barely speak English. He resolved not to fight with Tristant over the salad at supper that night, because that was supposed to be something else that sheepherders could not get in the hills.

The boy's sense of peace began to slip away when he saw Conchita stick her beak around the corner of the shed. Conchita belonged to the Columbo Hotel, but every once in a while she would flap her way over the high wooden fence to peck for worms where the ground stayed moist longer. She was wary because she expected to have a rock thrown at her. Pete did not disappoint Conchita. He threw the rock, but she ducked behind the shed just in time. Pete forgot her for the moment and went to the nail where he had tied the end of MacTavish's string.

MacTavish was a horny toad that Pete had found in the sagebrush outside the city limits. Pete had been afraid of MacTavish at first because he looked so ferocious with his horny covering, and had picked him up only on a dare. But MacTavish proved to be harmless and langorous, especially when his soft underbelly was scratched. In those moments, he would stretch out his legs and lie blissfully in Pete's palm.

Putting the flies into his shirt pocket, Pete sat down on the ground and began to pull in MacTavish's string. But only the slack came before he felt a tug on the other end of the string. The tug told Pete that something was wrong. MacTavish was too tiny to resist any kind of pull.

"I'll bet he went and got himself stuck behind the shed," Pete told himself. He got to his feet and went down the length of the string gently so as not to hurt MacTavish. He reached the shed and turned the corner.

At first, Pete could not believe what he was seeing. He closed his eyes and held them shut. When he opened them again, he knew his eyes had not deceived him. The end of the string led to Conchita's mouth and then disappeared. Nausea gripped Pete with an icy chill and his breakfast coffee was bitter in his mouth. Conchita cowered on the ground, but not from guilt. She was trapped like a fish on a hook.

Afterwards, Pete could not remember going berserk. The only things he remembered clearly were the chopping block and the feel of a hatchet in his hand. The rest of it came back in elusive snatches, Conchita snapping the string in her terror, the sound of flapping wings as she dodged the slashing blows, and Conchita clawing her way to the top of the fence.

Conchita must have been squawking and he must have been screaming, because his mother had burst out the door in her big white apron and was running toward him. She reached him as he was clambering over the fence in pursuit of Conchita. He felt the strong hands pinion his arms and set him down on the ground.

"What are you doing? Have you gone crazy?"

"God damn you! Leave me alone!"

And then lights exploded in his head. He reached up to touch his face. It was numb, and he realized he had been slapped. Pete raised his eyes to his mother's and knew that if he said one word, another slap was ready for him. The madness had dissipated and now his courage deserted him. He wilted and bowed his head and tasted injustice. She had not even bothered to ask why he had wanted to kill Conchita.

4

His brothers and sisters had been routed from the bedroom behind the kitchen and told to have their breakfast and go outside, so that Pete would be alone in his place of punishment. Sensing from their mother's expression that this time Pete had outdone himself, they dressed and left the room without saying a word to him. Only his baby sister, Michelle, had dared to look back once with tears in her eyes, and for that she received a spank on her bottom. Then his father had walked through on his way to shave. He must have heard what had happened, because he stared down at Pete from a great height with murder in his eyes. It was a look that Pete did not see often, but when he did, he felt the blood draining from his face and shivers course along his spine.

Because it would show if his father accosted him on the way back, Pete did not dare to begin plotting revenge. He waited until the sounds of the razor slapping against the strop, the scraping off of whiskers, and the hard pulling of the comb through iron black hair were done, and he hung his head while his father passed through again.

When he heard his father's muffled voice in the kitchen beyond, Pete went into his parents' bedroom. He knew exactly what he was going to do. On the dresser in the nearly bare room there was a metal box in which his mother kept the things that were private to her. Pete had come upon it one day by accident, not knowing what it was or what it contained. He had flipped open the top and seen that it was filled with such things as locks of baby hair tied with ribbons, letters written in a language he could not read, but which he supposed was Basque, and pictures of people he did not recognize. There was one picture, however, that seemed vaguely familiar to him.

It was of a young woman, almost a girl, leaning upon a pedestal. The arm that leaned on the pedestal was slender, and the hand that cupped the chin was fragile and white. The girl was more beautiful than anyone he had ever seen. She had a delicate face framed with soft black hair that was pulled upwards and kept in place by combs. But it was the eyes that held him most. They were huge and dark and wistful, and they concealed something that escaped him.

He had been about to put the picture back when he realized with happy surprise at first, and then with shock, that it was of his mother. He could not reconcile the girl in the picture with what his mother had become. The fragile hands had thickened and the slender arm was now grooved and muscled like a man's. Something of the delicate face remained, but the dark, wistful eyes were stern and hardened now.

Pete realized from that moment that he loved his mother. It was a secret he had never revealed by so much as a glance. It was a secret so guarded that he had never kissed his mother from that day on. And now, the revenge he had chosen was to destroy the picture.

Pete tiptoed past the iron bed to the dresser. Without remorse, he opened the box. His fingers knew exactly where the picture was, because he had last put it there himself. He jerked it out roughly and was about to tear it in two when the expression in the huge dark eyes caught him.

With stunning clarity, he saw what he had tried without success to see before. The eyes that looked out at him concealed a hurt so terrible that he felt his heart rip. Blinded by tears, he stuffed the picture back into the box and closed the lid.

Muted by distance, he heard the screen door to the kitchen slam shut and his sister Michelle's voice piping, "Mama! Mama! MacTavish is gone! I bet Conchita ate him."

You should have told me, his mother's eyes said when she came into the bedroom. *I would have understood.*

Pete wanted to tell her that she should have understood without words why he had gone crazy. She was his mother and by reason of that was supposed to know everything that went on in his mind. Then it came to him that this was not so, that there were things she could not know unless he told her. The knowledge opened up huge possibilities for secrecy in his life, but he was not sure he wanted that. The price of a secret, it seemed to him, was loneliness.

5

Pete had been released from his bedroom prison in time for the war. He would have felt badly about missing that, since his friend Tony and he had spent hours in plotting their battle plan. As it was, he was late and the two opposing armies were already drawn up in battle formation in front of the fortress, which was a deserted barn in the empty lot across the V & T railroad tracks from his parents' little hotel.

Predictably, Tony was ready to take on the enemy all by himself. His dark face did not betray his relief when Pete showed up, but the faces of the enemy showed disappointment that Pete had not chickened out. In an instant, the battle was met and the enemy engaged.

The encounter raged fearfully as Pete and Tony gained the threshold to the loft and even took Sonny Irish prisoner. Then the tide of battle turned.

Their shields beaten to a pulp by the downward force of the sword blows, Pete and Tony backed slowly down the ladder. When they reached the safety of the barn floor and looked up, it was to see three sweaty faces leering at them from the square hole that led to the loft.

The new kid, Rusty, called down to them in the slow southern drawl that always surprised Pete. "I guess we showed you guys. Y'all wanna call it a draw?"

"Draw is the wrong word," said Tony with irritation. "It's a truce."

"Who says so?" said Rusty.

"Pete does," said Tony. "He's the only one that's read the book."

"Who cares?" said Rusty, but added, "Anyway, y'all wanna call it a truce. It's hot up here."

"Tough shit," said Tony. "For all I give a damn, you can stay there until Hell freezes over."

Pete thrilled as Tony unlimbered his habit of swearing. He wondered if Tony could get away with cussing at the Orphans Home and decided that he could because everyone seemed to make allowances for Tony. There was some dark trouble in Tony's life, something that had to do with making him an orphan. When Tony was quiet and the dark thing showed in his eyes, Pete knew enough to leave him alone. In a while it would pass, and Tony would be Tony and his best friend again.

Because they were intrusive, Pete put thoughts of Tony out of his head and concentrated on his wound. His right arm smarted from one sword cut that had slid past his shield and caught him in the crook of the elbow. He consoled himself with the fact that wounds on head and arms didn't count. At least he had not been hit in the vital area between shirtcollar and belt, which would have meant he was dead.

Tony examined his shield ruefully. Because he had borne the brunt of the attack, his shield had taken the worst beating from the defenders of the fortress. One blow had sliced down through the cardboard all the way to the hand grip. Tony threw the shield aside and went to where their prisoner was standing morosely against the wall. Sonny Irish had been fooled by Tony's favorite trick, a backhand slash that looped over the enemy's head and then swept downward for the leg cut that meant you were prisoner. Sonny Irish was not much of a warrior. He always fell for the same trick.

"You got to give me your shield because you're a prisoner," said Tony.

"That ain't fair," Sonny Irish blustered. "I worked all yesterday on this shield. It's almost brand new."

"Tough shit," said Tony. "Pete says that's the rules, and he's the only one that's read the book."

"That's right," said Pete. "When a knight is taken prisoner, he has to surrender his weapons."

"It still ain't fair," said Sonny Irish belligerently.

"This prisoner has got to be taught a lesson," said Tony. "Lie down, Sonny. We got to hogtie you."

"I can't," said Sonny. "It's almost lunchtime."

Pete felt a surge of fury. Sonny Irish was always bringing up things that had nothing to do with war. Tony, who was a head taller than Sonny, loomed over him menacingly. "Lie down, prisoner."

After one look at Tony, Sonny Irish lay down on his stomach. Pete and Tony tied Sonny's hands behind his back, pulled his ankles forward and tied them with the same rope, so that his hands and feet were bound together. When that was done, they drew what was left of the rope across Sonny's throat and back to his legs.

"It's too tight," gasped Sonny. "I'm choking."

Tony relaxed the loop that passed across Sonny's throat. "Can you breathe now?"

"Yeah," said Sonny unhappily. "But you're gonna make me get a licking for being late to lunch."

There was a sudden clumping of shoes from the loft. The defenders were making a dash for freedom. Pete and Tony groped for their swords and shields. By the time they reached the ladder, three sets of legs were making a clambering descent from the loft.

"Revenge!" screamed Tony, cutting wildly at the enemy. Unable to protect their legs, the defenders never had a chance. Before they reached the bottom of the ladder, they had received the wounds that made them prisoners. After an hour of fighting, the battle had ended in the space of seconds.

"Well, war is like that," reflected Pete as he went out the fortress door. Waiting until Sonny Irish had been untied and the warriors had dispersed, he surveyed the battlefield alone. Lowering his shield, he placed the tip of his sword on the ground. Then he looked down to make sure his posture was correct, shield hanging loosely beside one leg, his other knee bent slightly, and the proper weariness in the incline of his body. It had been a satisfying war. The defenders had fought well, and it could have been touch and go there if they had succeeded in escaping from the siege of the tower.

Then Pete made the mistake of leaning heavily on his sword. The blade cracked in two, and so did his reverie. The battlefield became a dusty lot, the fortress an old barn, the sword only a wooden lathe. He threw it away in disgust and trudged homeward under the burning noonday sun, wondering why things never turned out the way they were supposed to, except in books.

6

The capitol dome was not much of a dome, but then Carson City was after all the smallest capital in the United States. This was drummed into the children of Carson from day one by townspeople and schoolteachers and the Carson City *Daily Appeal*. The children accepted the boast and repeated it to each other as dutifully as if it were one of the Commandments.

In Pete's heart, however, he did not think it was much of a distinction. And he suspected the townspeople did not really think so either, because there was always a note of chagrin around the edges of the voices that intoned it. He was to realize later that they were already beginning to think about bigness as a virtue.

Pete lay on his back in the yielding, sweet-smelling grass of the capitol grounds and watched the baffled sun trying to find a way through the leafy elms above his head. It was here on the capitol grounds that Pete found the liquid shade and grass and darkening green leaves of summer. Through his thin shirt he could feel the grass pushing outward from the cool earth beneath. He rubbed his shoulders deliciously against the thrusting blades and listened idly to the exclamations and moans from the mumbledepeg game going on behind him. Pete had won the game hands down, and now it was a question of who would lose and have to pick the tamped-in matchstick out of the grass with his teeth. He felt sure that the victim would be his kid brother, Mike, who never seemed to be able to get past spank-the-baby.

Beyond the circle of the mumbledepeg game, Buckshot Dooney was sleeping off a drunk. It must have been one beauty of a drunk, Pete reflected, because here it was afternoon and Buckshot was still asleep.

Pete turned over on his side and propped his hand against his head so he could observe the man. Buckshot was sprawled on his back and snoring, and his face that had been clean shaven for a month was now covered with the blackest stubble of beard Pete had ever seen. Buckshot was back in his old striped overalls, and the silk hat he had worn for the last month was replaced by the familiar battered derby. Pete remembered the freshly painted sign that announced Buckshot's latest endeavor. Something had gone wrong, he decided. Buckshot was for sure off the wagon again.

Buckshot seemed to travel from trouble to trouble. Within Pete's range of memory, Buckshot's brother had taken him into his furniture store business. But Buckshot's brother had kicked him right out again when he woke up one morning to find that Buckshot had sold most of his stock to his friends in the dead of night at giveaway prices. Buckshot's next endeavor had been to go around to the business places on main street selling orders for a new thing called linoleum. The business people paid, but they never saw. Out of work but not quite bereft, Buckshot had gone on a toot made memorable when he accosted an old girl friend who had gone on to marry a judge. She high-hatted Buckshot once too often, and he peed on her leg in front of the U.S. Mint. The judge had come looking for Buckshot with a horsewhip, but he had disappeared. A week later, when tempers had cooled, he came out again with the revelation that he had been hiding in an opium crib in the tunnels under Chinatown.

"O–U–T!" said Tony triumphantly, the dropping jackknife making a T with his extended finger and then imbedding itself in the grass. Pete turned briefly to observe his brother spitting out grass and dirt from digging out the matchstick with his teeth.

There was a sound of shoes flapping slowly on the sidewalk that led to the capitol building. Pete knew without turning over that it was George Washington Lopez on his way to wake up Buckshot. George Washington Lopez, whom everybody called Wash, was a stooped little man with rubbery lips, a mournful expression on his face, and the flattest feet in Carson City. He made his living swamping out the whorehouses a block away from the capitol.

When Wash came into view, Pete saw that he was hiding a bottle under his shabby coat. He veered unsteadily off the sidewalk and flapped his way toward his friend. Tony and Mike moved over and sat cross-legged beside Pete to watch the waking up of Buckshot.

"Buck! Hey, Buck!" mumbled Wash as he tried to prod Buckshot awake.

Buckshot was a long time in getting his eyes open. When he did, they wandered without recognition over the faces of his friend and the three boys.

"I brung you an eye opener, Buck," Wash said in a whisper that was louder than his speaking voice.

Buckshot first held out his hand and then with an effort of will drew himself up to a sitting position. Wash glanced covertly around and drew a bottle of beer out from under the folds of his coat. Buckshot regarded it disdainfully. "Jee-sus!" he said hoarsely. "At least you could've brought me the hair of the dog."

"Don't swear, Buck," said Wash in a pained voice. "You know taking the name of the Lord is a sin." He added as an afterthought, "It's the only thing Nigger Ruby would let me have. She's still got me on probation."

Pete knew the reason for that. The winter before, Nigger Ruby had given Wash money to buy firewood. Wash had turned the money to better uses. To cover himself, he had taken to stealing firewood at night from the back lot of Joe Rochamont's candy and cigar store. He got away with it for almost a month. Then Joe Rochamont, who had been a miner, bored some neat holes in a choice log and poured black powder into them. The log blew the roof off the whorehouse kitchen, and Wash was found out.

"Fuck Ruby," said Buckshot.

"Well," said Wash seriously. "That's her trade." Fumbling in his pocket, he drew out a bottle opener and uncapped the beer.

Buck drank thirstily, the beer trickling out of the corners of his mouth and finding its tortuous way through the black stubble of beard. He did not lower the bottle until it was empty, and then he belched and sighed. "It tastes like piss, but at least it's wet. Sit down, Wash, while I get my wits about me."

Wash sat down on the grass, shifted his weight until he was comfortable and then reached into a shirtpocket for his harmonica. Cupping it affectionately in his hands, he raised it to his mouth. The harmonica seemed to disappear between his lips. The music was sweet and soft. If nothing else, Wash could play *My Old Kentucky Home* better than anybody in town.

"That's nice, Wash," said Buckshot. He bent his head until the song was over. When he raised it again, he noticed the boys sitting cross-legged on the grass. An expression of shame came into his eyes. "I'm sorry, kids," he said. "I didn't mean for you to see me like this."

"What happened, Buck?" said Pete. "You been sober a long time."

"A run of bad luck, kids," said Buckshot. "They put me out of the undertaking business."

Pete did not know exactly who *they* were, but he could guess it had something to do with authority. He made a sound of sympathy. "That's too bad, Buck. You were doing pretty good with your Embalming on Easy Terms. People even said there may be some hope for you."

Buckshot shrugged. "Well, I *was* doing good. But the Chinamen did me in. Who would've thought they'd be the particular kind?"

Tony had not been much interested until now. "How could Chinks do you in? Nobody pays no mind to them."

"Well, this time they did," said Buckshot. He fumbled in the pencil pocket of his overalls for a cigar. Knowing that he would come up empty, Wash handed him a thin, twisted Mexican cigar. Buckshot grimaced but lighted it anyway. He inhaled tentatively, coughed and stuck the cigar in the corner of his mouth. "You boys remember that Chink who died a couple months ago in Chinatown?"

"Yeah," lied Pete so that he would not have to listen to one of Buckshot's long explanations.

"Well," said Buckshot. "When I got the message that a Chinaman had died and they wanted me to ship him back to China, I went out and made a nice Chink-sized coffin for him. That takes time and money, you know. Then, when the damned box was all ready, they brung me the corpse. And who does it turn out to be? The only six-foot Chinaman in Chinatown, if you can believe it."

Pete felt a tremor of anticipation course deliciously up his spine. Not daring to believe it himself, he whispered, "Did you make another coffin?"

Buckshot averted his gaze and stared sheepishly at the ground. "Well, let's just say I fixed him up and shipped him off to China."

"I don't get it," said Tony perplexedly. "How could you get a six-foot Chink in a Chink-sized box?"

"Aw, I don't want to talk about it," said Buckshot.

"We'll hear about it anyway, Buck," pleaded Pete.

Buckshot sighed. "I guess you're right. There's no secrets in this town. That's for sure." He took a deep puff on the cigar, let the smoke come out slowly, and confessed. "I cut him off at the knees."

"No!" cried Pete with horrified delight.

Tony's breath whistled out. "What did you do with the rest of him?"

Buckshot made an impatient gesture. "I didn't throw 'em away, if that's what you're thinking. I just laid those legs real nice alongside the corpse. He was all there, even if he wasn't in one piece. Who would ever have thought the government of China would get so mad about one Chinaman, when as everyone knows, there's millions of 'em starving to death over there."

Wash had been listening with disapproval. Though he must have heard the story the night before, or the night before that, considering the duration of Buckshot's binges, it was clear that Wash did not think Buckshot should be putting himself down before children. "You kids shouldn't think bad about Buck," he mumbled sadly. "If he hadn't taken to drink and cheating people, he could've been Governor. Everybody always said that about Buck."

"Aw, Wash," said Buckshot. But he was pleased nevertheless.

Pete watched as the two of them began to shuffle their way to Main Street, Buckshot in his battered derby and striped overalls and Wash with his shabby coat and flapping shoes. They did not see the Governor coming down the capitol steps in his high starched collar, with his overfed stomach stuck out in front of him. The three of them met at the sidewalk that led out of the capitol grounds. The Governor wrinkled his nose at the smell of whiskey that came off strongly from the saturated hides of Buckshot and Wash.

When they saw who it was, Buckshot and Wash stepped aside to let the Governor pass. Pete clamped his elbows against his side and prayed, *Buck, don't take off your hat. Please don't take off your hat!*

But Buckshot did.

7

With little Mike tagging behind, Pete and Tony made their way lazily down Main Street. At the Heroes Memorial Building they had stopped at the World War I cannon long enough to blast the capitol into rubble. At the big stone fountain that was a Pony Express marker, Pete and Tony had drunk first from the high, arching jets and then boosted Mike up so that he could drink, too. Pete had splashed water on Tony, and that had led to a water fight which left them drenched and refreshed from the afternoon heat.

The squaws had moved over to the shady side of the street, and Pete bent down to peek into the dark caverns that the blankets formed over their heads, catching glints of black eyes in wooden faces marked with blue lines. At Sam the butcher's sawdust-floored market, they thrust their heads into the cool interior and stared hungrily at the red ropes of hot dogs hung over pegs. Pete fingered the two pennies in his pocket and almost succumbed to the temptation. He was tempted again when they stood in agony before Kelly and Linsey's bakery and its display of doughnuts covered with a sugar glaze, but he shook his head and tore himself away.

In front of Bergen's pool hall, they stopped to have a consultation. Pete's two pennies were all the money there was between them. Little Mike could not be expected to have any money, and Tony had only the two square nails he was saving for the coming of the train. Pete decided to compromise, and they went into the pool hall to spend one penny for three Red Hot Dollar candies.

It was a while before Dutch could serve them. The *Reno Evening Gazette* had come in from that incomprehensibly big town of 20,000 people thirty miles away, and the men in the pool hall were lined up at the bar rolling the newspapers into tight bundles and then bending them in the middle so that they would not unroll when thrown onto doorsteps. Pete waited impatiently for the job to be done and beer to be served to the men, one glass for each one who helped.

Dutch took pity on Pete and interrupted his work at the foaming beer spigot to hand him the three Red Hot Dollars and collect his penny. Pete and Tony and Mike retired to the back of the pool hall to suck at their candy and watch the high school boys, who were not old enough to roll papers and get a free beer, play at rotation pool. But when Ned

Fotherwill came in and the commotion started, they forgot the pool and sidled along the wall to watch.

As people said, Ned Fotherwill was not exactly a lunatic, but he was sure as hell crazy. He lived with his brother, Ray, in a shack somewhere on the edge of town. And once a month, Ray would bring Ned into town to amuse himself for a day.

Ned had no sooner come in the door when one of the men standing at the bar shouted, "Hey, Ned! Sing us one of them songs that's made you famous the world over."

Flushing with pleasure, Ned Fotherwill stepped into the middle of the floor, cleared his throat and began singing "Little Red Fox" in a thin, quavering voice. When he was done, the men at the bar applauded and one of them said, "Well now, Ned. Sing us *another* song!" Ned bowed and grinned a toothless grin and began to sing. The song was "Little Red Fox."

After the fourth request and the fourth singing of "Little Red Fox," the men at the bar were laughing themselves silly. But Ned did not seem to hear. His face was wet with perspiration and he was trembling in ecstacy.

"Well now, Ned!" the same man said. "Give us something from an opera. How about that tune they built a statue of you in Salt Lake City for?"

Ned was a little taken aback by the mention of a statue. His brows furrowed and then cleared. "That's right. They did build a statue of me in Salt Lake City. I remember that now." He struck an operatic pose and thrust his arms out. "My arms were like this, and my mouth was open like this." And Ned opened his mouth.

"That's right, Ned!" said another man. "The people love that statue, but the pigeons like it better. It's not often they get a chance to shit in someone's mouth."

When it started, Pete had been almost hysterical with laughter. Now, suddenly the baiting of Ned Fotherwill was not funny anymore. His face mirroring his disgust, he poked Tony with his elbow in a signal that he wanted to leave. But before he could, he felt a big hand on his shoulder. When he looked up, it was to see the kindly face of Ray Fotherwill.

"Don't take it so hard, boy," Ray said to Pete. "If Ned was all right in the head, I would take offense myself. But he's crazy. All he will remember is that people asked him to sing. So what the hell, son?"

8

The pool hall and the plight of poor Ned Fotherwill were driven out of Pete's mind by his predicament. The afternoon whistle of the Virginia & Truckee Railway train, lonely with distance, caught them clinging by their fingertips to the rough stone siding of the abandoned U.S. Mint.

Looking back along the thin ledge to their starting point near the front of the building, Pete realized with panic that there would not be enough time to retrace their steps. He peeked over his shoulder at the ground below, and his stomach sank. It seemed an impossible distance down.

Reading his thoughts, Tony went through the same motion that Pete had, peering over his shoulder at the ground below. He swallowed visibly. Over the head of little Mike, who was hanging to the wall between them, his eyes met Pete's.

"We got to jump," hissed Pete. "It's the only way we can make it on time."

"Okay," said Tony. "But you go first."

More at the terror in Tony's voice than his words, little Mike began to wail. "It's too far! I'm afraid!"

"We'll figure out a way to get you down," said Pete. But little Mike did not believe him and wailed louder.

"Shut up, you old scaredy cat," said Pete, and jumped. As he flew through space, he twisted his body around so that he would not roll into the building when he hit ground. The shock was the worst he had ever known, starting from the soles of his feet and jarring its way up his spine and whipping his head forward. He lay doubled up on the ground, making hideous noises as he fought to suck air back into his lungs.

"Are you dying?" Tony called down hoarsely.

Pete sat up and felt his legs. They were not broken into pieces as he had expected. "It's easy," he said to Tony. "Come on down." He stood aside sadistically to watch Tony's descent.

Clapping his hands over his eyes, Tony tottered on the ledge and fell. Because he could not see the ground coming up to meet him, he landed and rolled once and was on his feet almost in the same motion. He glanced superiorly at Pete. "Easy as pie," he said. "What were you making all those dying sounds for?"

Pete ignored him on the pretense of thinking up a plan to get Mike off the ledge. "I got an idea," he said. "I'll get on your shoulders and he can shinny down both of us."

Tony braced himself against the wall and Pete climbed up his back until he was standing on Tony's shoulders. "You could've taken your shoes off," Tony complained. Pete did not hear him. He was trying to talk Mike into letting go of the wall and shinny down. Mike would not let go even under the threat of being left on the ledge all night. Finally, Pete reached up and grasped Mike's legs and tore him loose. For an instant, the entire column wavered and almost collapsed. Then Mike caught a handhold in Pete's hair. Pete set his teeth against the pain, and little Mike began the descent.

The whistle of the V & T sounded again, dangerously close to town. Galvanized into action, they gained the sidewalk and finding it too filled with people going home from work, veered into the uncrowded street. They skirted under the nose of Bill Muldoon's old buggy horse, surprising her so much that she reared in her traces for the first time in memory. A Model T coming from the other direction tooted its horn angrily as they passed in front. They added insult to injury by outdistancing it. From then on, it was clear sailing.

When they reached the depot, it was to see the black, steaming hulk of the V & T already at the city limits on its daily run to Reno. Dodging the rumbling handcarts pushed by men in black cloth arm gauntlets and little caps, they streaked across the wooden platform to the tracks. With trembling hands, Pete placed his penny and Tony his nails on the track. The V & T let go an ear-splitting blast of warning and they leaped back onto the platform. The engine rumbled dutifully over the penny and nails and came to a stop with a great hiss of steam. Mike arrived in time to stand with Pete and Tony in the wet boiler-smelling vapor that rose up around them like clouds. From his high seat, the engineer in his cap and red bandanna wagged a finger and shouted something incomprehensible.

When the steam had evaporated, they went to the side of the depot to begin their patient wait for the train's departure. Old man Castle, who had been retired from the railroad, was there as always to observe the coming and going of the train with watery eyes and a sad, lost face. Sam the butcher had come down the street to watch, too. Oblivious of the grimaces of the boys, he stood wiping his hands on his blood-smeared apron.

"Oh Christ! Those bastards again," Sam muttered aloud, and Pete turned his head to see whom Sam the butcher was talking about.

Two men in business suits and snap-brim hats were getting off the train. Their faces were stern and intent, and they glanced suspiciously to the right and left as they stepped onto the platform. One of them was thin, with wire-rimmed glasses and a bitter mouth, as if he had tasted something bad.

Sam the butcher noticed Pete for the first time. He leaned over and said ominously into Pete's ear. "You better tell your folks the Prohis are in town." He turned to go and whispered back conspiratorially, "I'll pass the word downtown."

Pete felt his face freeze and the breath catch in his throat. He did not know what the word Prohi stood for, but he knew that it was a word filled with terror and ruin and nightmares of jail. Without a word to Tony, he grasped Mike by the hand and fled over the depot platform and out into the street.

When they reached the hotel, Tristant the sheepherder was standing out in front. Tristant was in good humor. He tried to tease Pete by blocking the doorway. Pete screamed at him and Tristant stood aside, his expression gone sober with the awareness of trouble. When they were inside the hotel, Pete let go of little Mike and ran down the length of the long dining room. The table was already set for the boarders' dinner, and there were wine glasses in front of each plate. Pete scooped up two of the wine glasses on his way through the swinging doors.

The kitchen was sweltering and his mother's face was wet with perspiration when she turned away from the stove. Whatever she was going to say to him for his noisy entrance was stilled when she saw the wine glasses he was holding.

"Prohis!" Pete gasped.

His mother's hand went to her head and her body swayed as if she were going to faint. Then, with an effort of will that shook her frame like a leaf in the wind, she straightened. "Inside?"

Pete shook his head. "Depot!"

Her eyes closed and fluttered open again. "Lock the front door," she said, and then thought better of it. "No! Go tell your father!" Gathering up her long white apron, she ran into the dining room. Pete waited until he heard her footsteps stop. When the lock on the front door clicked shut, Pete took the back route through the bedrooms into the saloon. His big brother, Leon, was sprawled on a bed and his two sisters were playing jacks on the floor. He paused only long enough to shout, "Prohis! Put the wine glasses away!" He caught one glimpse of Leon raising himself bolt upright on the bed and the blanching faces of his sisters, and then Pete was gone through the back door.

His father, black haired and tall, was standing behind the high old bar in the saloon, serving whiskey in shot glasses to a few politicians and Mizoo, the big cowboy with the ten-gallon hat. Pete was not afraid of Mizoo, but he was intimidated by the politicians in their suits and neckties and shined, knobby shoes. He stood in the doorway, trying to catch his father's attention. It was a while before his father recognized the agonized plea in Pete's face. He left the group at the bar and stood over Pete. "What's the matter?"

"Prohis!" Pete whispered.

"Why didn't you say so?" his father said fiercely. He took two long steps to the bar and spoke in low warning. As one, the men downed their shots of whiskey and passed through the intervening door into the dining room. Pete's father rinsed out the glasses and put them away in a drawer. Whipping the bottle of whiskey off the bar, he corked it and went into the bathroom. Pete heard the splash of the bottle sinking into the water cabinet on the wall high above the toilet and went limp with relief. The peremptory knocking by the Prohis on the front door of the hotel did not bother him. They were safe now.

9

It was the strangest dinner Pete could ever remember. The boarders sipped their soup grumpily and with little conversation. His mother served the rich beef stew, apologizing to the boarders and muttering that it was a scandal to serve a French dinner like this without wine. Tristant the sheepherder nodded in solemn agreement. His father sat at the head of the table, scowling and speaking to no one.

The Prohis came back when the stew was being served. They looked thwarted and angry, and they were almost rude when they asked Pete's mother if they could eat dinner. Pete glanced apprehensively toward the head of the table. His father's hands were clenched into fists beside his plate and the murderous look was in his eyes again. He might have done something violent if Pete's mother had not put her hand warningly on his shoulder.

Neither the big cowboy, Mizoo, nor Mickey McCluskey, who was an old prospector, were to be put off so easily. Mizoo at least had had his shot of whiskey before dinner, but Mickey McCluskey had arrived too late, and he felt his loss sorely. A puckish gleam of revenge shone in his eyes.

"What a terrible thing it is, this goddam Prohibition," he said in his Irish brogue. "A man can't even wash the dust out of his throat properly after a hard day's work. It's the saddest thing in town, I'm telling ye."

Aghast, Pete leaned over to peek at the Prohis. Both of them had stiffened, and the thin one with the wire-rimmed glasses looked as if he had heard blasphemy.

Mizoo set down his knife and fork carefully on his plate. His eyes met Mickey McCluskey's across the table, and then narrowed. "Well, there's some as knows how to get all the booze they wants," he drawled.

"Ye don't say!" said Mickey McCluskey.

"I do say," said Mizoo.

"And where would that be, lad?"

"Not in a house like this," drawled Mizoo. "It's a respectable place. Downright too respectable for my tastes."

"We all know that," said Mickey McCluskey. "But you're not answering my question."

"Well, I hear tell," drawled Mizoo, "the ones who got all the booze are the Prohis."

There was a clatter of a fork from the end of the table, but Pete did not dare look. Keeping his eyes riveted on his plate, he pretended not to hear what was going on.

"That makes sense," said Mickey McCluskey. "Indeed it do. But how does one go about getting acquainted with them Prohi boys?"

"Aw, that's easy," said Mizoo. "You just keep your eyes peeled for a Presbyterian whose face says he's out to reform the world. You can spot 'em every time."

"And what d'ye do when you've spotted one?" said Mickey McCluskey innocently.

"You just get 'em aside and make your proposition."

"D'ye mean offer them money?" said Mickey McCluskey. "That don't seem to me to be hardly legal."

"Aw!" said Mizoo. "Everybody knows that's how they make their money. They make a raid, they sell the booze."

There was a harsh scraping of chairs on the wooden floor, and this time, Pete dared to look. The two Prohis were on their feet. One of them was putting money for the dinner on the table, and the other, the one with the wire-rimmed glasses, looked as if he were going to be sick. His mouth worked like a fish out of water and then he said in a constricted voice, "We will have you know that we are Presbyterian agents." He faltered, "I mean Prohibition agents."

"Ye don't say!" said Mickey McCluskey, his eyes alight as if in genuine surprise. "Pleased to have ye with us, I'm sure. And would ye be telling me if you've got some booze for sale? I'll make ye a fair offer, I'm that thirsty."

Pete did not watch the Prohis leave. He was staring at Mickey McCluskey and Mizoo, unashamed of the worship he knew was in his eyes.

10

Mickey McCluskey and Mizoo had done for the Prohis in their fashion at dinner, but Pete still needed to strike a blow against the government before the day ended, for what it had made his mother suffer.

Since it was a family affair, he had tried to recruit his big brother, Leon, as his accomplice. Leon, whom their mother considered the only one in the family with no nonsense in his head, had argued that the Prohis were federal government and Pete's intended victim was state government, which didn't have anything to do with Prohibition.

Pete had shouted at him that it was *all* government, federal or state, and that it was *his* mother, too, who had suffered, but Leon had walked away saying the whole idea was pretty silly. So Pete had recruited Tony, who didn't have to have revenge explained to him.

It was dusk and they were huddled like conspirators behind the trunk of an elm that was black and bleeding with summer sap. They had made their way there by a devious route, creeping along the iron fence with its spear-tipped points, following the night shade of other elms, and sprinting across those patches of open grass that the moonlight had gotten to.

All that lay between them and the capitol's big doors was a short stretch of sidewalk and a flight of stone steps. On his hands and knees, Pete crept along the sidewalk and up the stone steps. When he reached the doors, he raised himself up just enough to peer over the dividing line between wood and glass. In order to see through the glass, he had to cup his hands alongside his eyes like a horse with blinkers. They were in luck and he dropped down again and waved his arm to Tony in a signal.

They edged through one of the doors, and Pete said quiet thanks in his heart to the janitor who had finally gotten around to oiling the hinges. But he was also afraid now for the first time, because of the presence of the white-haired watchman at the crossing of the corridors. The fact that the watchman was asleep with his chair tipped back against the wall did not allay Pete's fears, because after all he was a man with a man's hard hands and if he woke up too soon, there would be the dickens to pay.

But the watchman did not wake up until they had made it on tiptoe to the crossing of the corridors. They turned the corner undetected and saw in front of them the long corridor with marble floors and marble walls gleaming in the half light. The corridor stretched invitingly all the long way to the other doors at the side entrance.

Pete knew the watchman would come awake in a hurry when they started to run, but that was unimportant now. They poised themselves like sprinters. "Go!" hissed Pete, and they went. The leather heels that they had supplemented with brass taps cracked with the staccato rattle of machine gun fire, and the echoes bounced with purest ecstasy off the marble walls.

The worry of the watchman was behind them, but there was another obstacle to pass, and Tony shouted out in a strangled voice, "Don't look! Don't look!"

But that was the best insurance that they would look. And both of them turned their heads and looked upwards at the dead old man with a long gray-streaked beard and furious eyes staring down out of the dark oil portrait where he had been fixed in time. With moans of fear, they hurled themselves against the doors and scrambled into the safety of the night.

By the time they had fled down the sidewalk and through the aperture in the iron fence, they had forgotten their fear. The dark expanse oɪ grass and trees, the domed fortress of stone, the fearful portrait of a dead old man Governor, and even the night watchman's hoarsely-shouted threats of things to come were all behind them now, and could hurt them no longer.

When they parted, Tony at a trot because it was past curfew at the Orphans Home, Pete sauntered casually down Main Street to the little hotel, reflecting on the day.

It had been long and puzzling. But at least it had started out right with the sunrise and ended right with the coming of darkness and his blow against authority. He sensed now that vengeance was a part of his makeup that he could do nothing about, but he was not sure whether he liked that. Everything else could bear thinking about when he was in bed. Somewhere within Pete, he felt a vague awareness of lessons learned and a premonition that he was beginning to discover his world.

11

Pete had exhausted the possibilities in the cottonwood trees that grew outside the tall windows. With his chin cupped in his hand, he had watched the lowering light of afternoon work its changes on the big leaves and then took to examining individual leaves to see how far the gold had pushed its way into the green.

After that, he had slumped back in his seat and regarded the array of Halloween figures with which Victor, the best artist in school, had covered two panels of the blackboard on the side of the classroom. To Pete's mind, they were as good as anything in the funnies: witches with peaked hats and warty noses and missing teeth, who really did frighten, and goblins with round bellies and green faces and impish smiles, who did not frighten a bit.

Reaching into his desk, Pete took out a tablet and a pencil and tried to copy the ones he liked. He had more success with the witches because their expressions were uniformly evil, but the goblins frustrated him because he could not capture the subtle mix of evil and glee. Giving it up as a bad job, he tore the sheet from the tablet and crumpled it angrily.

The crackling of the paper made a sound that was unbelievably loud in the silent classroom. Miss Benton looked up from her desk at the front of the room, fixed him for an instant with a vexed look, and went back to correcting papers. Fascinated by the noise the paper had made, Pete decided to listen to the silence. He heard sounds he had never heard before—the ticking of the big clock, the creaking of floors, and the whispered settling of stone walls—and from somewhere far away, the muffled coughing of Mr. Quill, who was the janitor and who people said had something called TB. When he listened harder, Pete could hear the rustling of Mr. Quill's broom as he pushed it down the length of the hallway. There was another sound, too, but this one did not make any sense. It was a quiet, cautious shifting as of feet, and it seemed to come from behind the door of the cloakroom where the kids hung their coats. The unexplained sound sent a shiver up Pete's back and he looked apprehensively at the door to the cloakroom. The sound did not repeat itself.

Miss Benton sighed, and Pete took to examining her. It occurred to him that he had never really seen her before. Gone were the firmness and the animation by which he knew her through the school day. There were deep furrows between her eyes and her face sagged, and Pete realized with astonishment that she was tired. Against his will, because after all she had kept him after school, he felt a pang of pity for her.

When the clock struck five and she raised her head, the firmness returned as if by magic to her features. "All right, Pete," she said. "You can go home now." She regarded him for a moment as if gathering her strength. "But I warn you. The next time you get in a fight in school, the principal will strap you."

Pete had a brief vision of the obscene razor strop in the principal's office, and of the principal himself, a stern man with erect military bearing. "No, he won't."

Miss Benton's eyes widened. "What did you mean by that?"

"I didn't start the fight, Miss Benton. Jimmy Secombe did. He called me a name."

"What did he call you?"

Pete reddened. "Nothing." He turned away in confusion to gather up his books.

"Well, that's your private affair, Pete," Miss Benton said, and by the tone in her voice, Pete understood that she knew what the name was. Whatever pity he had felt for her vanished. She was on the other side, too.

Miss Benton rose from her desk as Pete stalked toward the cloakroom to get his coat. "Pete," she called softly. But when he did not stop, she said commandingly, "Pete!"

He turned toward her grudgingly, but hung his head so that he would not have to meet her eyes.

"What does that have to do with the principal?" Miss Benton said.

Pete raised his head. "Because he heard what Jimmy Secombe called me, and Jimmy Secombe didn't get punished."

Miss Benton sighed, and there was more than weariness in her voice. "I'm sorry, Pete. I didn't know."

But Pete had turned away and was opening the cloakroom door. The welcome darkness flooded over him. He stood for a moment trying to control his breathing, and then groped for his Mackinaw jacket. He jerked it off its hook and jumped back in fright. Someone was huddled in the corner of the cloakroom.

Pete's nose told him who it was before his eyes did. "Romy! You scared me."

The Indian boy's eyes were so big that the whites showed. "I didn't mean to," he mumbled.

Miss Benton appeared in the doorway to the cloakroom. "What's going on in there? Who are you talking to, Pete?"

Romy crept out of his corner and stood with bent head before Miss Benton. He was wearing only a tattered shirt and pants and he gave off a powerful unwashed odor.

"Why, Romy!" Miss Benton said. "You're shaking. Is there anything the matter?"

Romy shook his head but did not lift his eyes.

"Romy," said Miss Benton. "Tell me why you were hiding in the cloak-room."

But Romy stood mute, and Miss Benton knew he was not going to tell her anything. "Well, get your coat and go home," she said. "It's late."

"He doesn't have a coat," said Pete. "He's an Indian and so he's poor."

Miss Benton cleared her throat. "Both of you get out of here," she said in a voice that was not successfully harsh.

"Come on, Romy," said Pete. "Let's go home." Ashamed to put on his Mackinaw jacket, he carried it in one arm and draped the other over Romy's thin shoulders. They walked along the dim hallway, and Pete noticed the rim of light under the principal's door and wrinkled his nose at it. When they got to the big front doors of the schoolhouse, Pete felt Romy hanging back. "What's the matter, Romy?"

"Nothing," said Romy. He shook off Pete's arm, took a deep shuddering breath, and then darted through the doorway and down the steps as if he were being pursued.

He was. They had been hiding behind the corner of the school building and they caught him before he was across the schoolyard. There were three of them, high school boys who were big and strong and on the football team. One of them left his feet in a flying tackle, and Romy went down in a flurry of fists and kicks and hoarse oaths of dirty Indian and goddam Washoe.

It had all happened too quickly. Paralyzed, Pete stood on the top of the steps and watched Romy go down. It was not until the beating up was well along that Pete shook himself free of shock and ran to help

Romy, and then it was too late. Pete's fists struck empty air as one of Romy's attackers kept him at bay with a long arm. Another one delivered a last kick at Romy's curled-up form.

"Bastards!" screamed Pete.

They gathered ominously around him, and surrounded by their bulk, Pete knew fear. "You better shut up or you'll get it next," said one of them. "Goddam little shit of a bootlegger."

When they were gone, Pete went to where Romy was sitting on the ground. His thin arms were scraped raw and the lumps were already beginning to rise on his cheekbones. There were tears in his eyes, but he had not made one sound throughout the beating up. He made no sound now, either, but sat staring at the ground while his chest heaved with the effort of gulping air into his lungs.

Pete took him by the arm. "Come on, Romy. Let's go home."

Romy looked up at him then with hatred in his eyes. "Leave me alone," he mumbled, and got up unsteadily and limped away, holding his arms across his stomach.

Pete watched him go and then trudged back to pick up his jacket and his books. There was a light in a window of the schoolhouse and Pete raised his eyes to it. The erect figure of the principal was framed in the window. He had been watching all the time.

12

The bitter aftertaste of disillusionment with men such as the principal soured his mouth. Pete did not relish the prospect of going to hear another man of position, a U.S. Senator from Nevada, talk.

But there was no way out of it. His mother had told their father to go for Leon's sake. She really meant *her* sake. It had become clear to Pete that she had some pretty big ambitions for Leon, which Pete thought were ridiculous. He would never have dared to voice his opinion and nobody would have paid attention anyway. Pete was sent along to accompany his father and Leon as punishment for fighting at school. His mother had no worries about Pete's becoming infected with ambition.

Autumn and election time were mingled one with the other in their lives because Carson City was a capital. They did not seem to go together, because one was a time of melancholy and the death of all green things and the other was a time of noise and fearful arguing.

Pete and his brother Leon were hurrying with their father and the others who were also late across the darkening main street toward the sound of a blaring band that threatened to burst the worn wooden sidings of the American Legion hall. It was sunset and the western sky was painted with long, uncertain bands of red. The light that filtered through the bands was red, too, so that the street was suffused with warmth and color.

In one instant, Pete's lungs were filled with the sharp dry smell of leaves dying on the great cottonwoods and the sentinel poplars. And in the next instant, they were filled with the mustiness of old boards, of the mothball-smelling suits of miners come to town, of buckaroos reeking with whiskey, of Indians and the bitter scent of sagebrush, of the hard unwashed sweat of working men that really mounted up to something by the Friday before the Saturday night bath.

By the time they got inside and found a standing place against the wall, the band had fallen quiet and a man was speaking. He was poised on a stage that was dazzling with red, white, and blue bunting and flags and huge swatches of butcher paper bearing his name and that of the Democratic party.

Pete nudged his brother. "Is that the Senator?"

"Yeah," said Leon. "Shut up and listen."

Pete regarded the Senator more closely. He was a slender man with a fine face and bearing. But at this moment, he was having some trouble with his bearing. Every time he made a grand gesture with one hand, he had to reach out with the other and hold onto a table that wobbled uncertainly beside him. The Senator was talking about silver, but that did not interest Pete at all. Instead, he was fascinated by the spindly legs of the table and what would happen if they suddenly collapsed under the pressure of the Senator's clutching hand. It was a time of torment for Pete because he wanted it to happen and not to happen, because he knew this man was proud.

Pete was released from his dilemma by an incident that diminished the affair of the table. The Senator made one flourish grander than the rest and his coat burst open in front. There as plain as day was revealed the butt end of a pistol stuck in his waistband. Around him, Pete heard the gasps of women and the guffaws of men.

The Senator was not at all embarrassed. "Ladies and gentlemen," he said. "You have nothing to fear, *because you are my friends.* I have carried this piece of hardware from the time I was a boy in the deep South until I became a man in the hard life of the Klondike. And I will continue to carry it until my dying day, because a man in politics is not without enemies."

Then the Senator laughed and said in a rich, fulsome drawl, "Anyway, I am the one who is taking the risk. Because if that thing should ever go off, its business end canted the way it is, I will never be the man I was before." And the women covered their faces with scandalized pleasure and the men stomped their feet and shook the hall with their laughter.

Afterwards, they made their way with their father back across the main street, filled now with the biting gasoline fumes of Model A's and Model T's and the clip clop of horse-drawn buggies and single saddle-horses and people on foot all moving together in a fluid stopping and starting and turning aside.

"Is the Senator really a drunk?" Leon asked their father.

Pete caught his breath, but their father did not get angry. He was silent for a moment, and then he said, "I don't know if he is a drunk or not. If he was, I wouldn't tell it to you. But I will tell you one thing. Politics to my mind is more talking than doing. And there is no man who can talk as good as him when he is drunk."

Pete pondered his father's words and decided he would have to figure them out later. Made bold by his brother's directness, Pete blurted, "Papa, are we bootleggers?"

"Shut up!" said Leon in choking fury. In the midst of all the noise in the street, Pete felt a ringing silence enclose him. He cowered, waiting for his father's wrath to come down on his head.

"It's a pretty night," his father said. "Let's walk a little."

They changed their direction and walked down Main Street toward the outskirts of town, passing business places and then homes with open porches. Their father did not speak until they had gone beyond the last street light. Beyond that, there was a wall of darkness broken only by far-scattered lights from an outlying ranch house or a forlorn Indian shack. But when they raised their eyes, because their father had done so first, they saw the sky blazing with the stars of an autumn night, and beyond, the black mass of the Sierra rearing into the purple night sky.

"Your mother and I was rich once, you know," their father said. "Then the livestock crash came and we lost everything. One day, we had a fancy house, and the next day we was broke and living in a shack with dirt for a floor. It wasn't a nice thing to happen, I can tell you." He turned suddenly and they began retracing their steps back into town. "For my part," he said as they walked, "living in a shack didn't bother me all that much. Because when I came to this country, I didn't have a thing except the clothes on my back. But your mother was raised different in the old country. She came from a family with property. I can't figure out why she came in the first place, because she sure didn't need to."

They were passing a house where a man and his wife were rocking back and forth on their front porch. Their father touched his hand to his hat. "How do," he said, and there was an answering murmur from the dark porch.

When they had gone on, their father said, "This little hotel, the one you live in now, came up for sale because the man who owned it got put in jail for bootlegging."

His breath catching, Pete turned to see if they were out of earshot of the man and his wife rocking on their porch. The movement did not escape his father, and he bent his head as if to say, *It's that bad, is it?* Pete's cheeks burned in shame, but this time it was because he had betrayed his father.

"We had one hundred dollars that your mother had saved up from cooking on ranches after we went broke," their father went on. "She made a down payment on the hotel and started taking in roomers and cooking for boarders. Because it was Prohibition and she was afraid, we didn't have no booze in the place at all. At first, it worked out all right, because she is one damned fine cook. Then we started to lose business. The people who was coming for dinners just didn't come back no more. We couldn't pay our bills. We was flat broke for the second time. We couldn't make the payments on the hotel, and it looked like we was going to have to get out. Your mother got desperate because you kids finally had a home and your little friends."

They were passing by the train depot now and nearing the hotel. Their father stopped and waved his hand in the direction of the depot. "I had a suspicion what was going wrong," he said. "So one afternoon I walked over there when the train was coming in. The sheriff was there, and when the people got off the train, he would tell them where to go for dinner. It wasn't to our place. So I walked up to him and I asked him why he was sending people to the other places in town. And he told me, 'Listen. The day you start serving booze, I can tell them to come to your place, because booze is what they are looking for.' I said to him, 'But it's against the law.' And he said, 'It's a crazy law and everybody except the Presbyterians knows it's a crazy law.' "

Their father's voice was bitter. "I can't figure this country out," he said. "If you don't serve people booze, you go broke. And if you do serve it, you get into trouble." They made their way to the front of the hotel, and then he said, "If giving people a little wine for dinner and a couple shots of whiskey beforehand is being a bootlegger, then I guess we are bootleggers."

They went into the hotel and their father locked the door after them. The long dining room was in gloom, but there was a light on in the kitchen where their mother was stacking dishes for breakfast. "Where did you go?" she said without looking up.

"For a little walk," their father said. He took off his coat and turned back the cuffs of his shirt to start taking the dishes out to the long table.

She looked up then, and without being told, knew exactly what the little walk had been about. A shadow crossed her face, and for the first time, Pete saw again the girl in the photograph. He felt a tugging in his chest, and for one terrible instant thought the hated tears were going to rise up to his eyes.

Leon went up to their mother and took her kiss. "Goodnight, Mama," he said, his face sober.

Pete ducked his head and stalked through the kitchen into the bedroom without saying goodnight. He was in flight.

W · I · N · T · E · R

13

Beverly Schultz had started it by raising her hand and saying, "Miss Benton, may I change my seat. I think I'm getting sick."

"Yes, Beverly," said Miss Benton. "I understand."

After that, everyone within two rows of Pete had raised their hands and been given permission to change their seats. Tony had stuck to the last, and then he, too, had given up and moved to the other side of the room, but not before hissing in Pete's ear, "Jesus H. Christ! What've you got on your boots?"

Pete sat alone in the corner of the room, surrounded by empty seats while the offending fumes rose up around him. He sat without moving, transfixed in immobility, not daring to raise his eyes above the level of the desk. He had never known such humiliation. He wished that he were invisible. He wished that death would strike him like a thunderbolt so that he would not have to face his classmates again.

"Donald," said Miss Benton weakly to the boy who was room monitor, "would you open the window near . . ." She paused out of delicacy, and added, "in the corner of the room."

But all that accomplished was to give the icy winter wind a chance to flow over the outcast and wash the fumes to the peopled side of the room. Beverly Schultz started it again. "Miss Benton," she said, "may I leave the room? I'm really sick now."

Miss Benton, who was looking a little green herself, said in a wavering voice, "Yes, Beverly. If any of the rest of you need to go to the restroom, you have my permission." She was struck with an idea. "In fact, why don't we go out to recess early today? Class dismissed!" She fled from the room ahead of her students. A clatter of footsteps followed her out, and Pete was suddenly by himself.

Deserted, he cursed the book he had been reading about the Yukon. In preparation for tomorrow's adventure, he had read the book so carefully, noting down all the preparations a man must make before setting out into the wilderness. The book had made a strong point about saturating one's boots with oil to keep out the wet. He had searched the kitchen of the hotel for oil, and had found only one bottle. Somehow, his eyes had fastened on the word *oil* and slid over the word before, which was *castor*. Now, he was trapped, afraid to go out and suffer the taunts of his friends, and worse, the girls' disdainful stares.

He was saved in an unexpected way. The principal had heard the clatter of feet and come in to find out why recess had been declared early. He stood in the doorway, his broad shoulders filling it from jamb to jamb. His angry stare lighted on Pete, and he strode forcefully to him.

"Where is your teacher?" he said in a stern voice.

Pete shrugged and did not answer.

"Stand up!" the principal said, his voice rising. "Where is your teacher?"

Pete stood up with hanging head. "She had to excuse herself," was all that he could think of to say.

The principal reached forward and chucked Pete's chin up sharply. "Look at me when you answer! What do you mean she had to excuse herself?"

A chance draft of cold wind came in the window, over the radiator, down to Pete's boots and up again. The principal took one breath and stepped back, realization dawning upon him. The hard lines of his face were melting with queaziness. "What have you got on your boots?"

"Castor oil," Pete said miserably.

"Castor oil!" the principal cried.

"To keep the wet out," said Pete.

The principal started to take a deep breath and then thought better of it. He definitely was not looking well, Pete reflected.

The principal mustered his strength. "You're excused for today. Go home and use the strongest soap you can find to scrub that . . ." He paused, searching for a word. ". . . medicine off your boots."

Pete gathered up his books, bound them with a strap, and trailed off to the cloakroom to get his jacket. The principal was opening every one of the big windows, and the cold was pouring in in great draughts. Pete hoped Beverly Schultz would freeze to death.

14

He was sitting in the empty gallery, but unobtrusively so that the Sergeant at Arms would not see him. The Sergeant at Arms had replaced the night watchman as his enemy in the capitol.

Pete had not come in because he was interested in what was being accomplished below. Because of the castor oil, he had an afternoon that was free. Also, there was snow and cold outside and he had come in for the blessed steam heat that hissed out of the radiators. But while he was there, it was also amusing to listen to old men argue.

Pete had been to the legislature enough times now to know something of what was going on. Not about the laws, which bored him, but about the men who were making them.

There was a man standing on his feet and arguing furiously about something having to do with THE SOVEREIGN STATE OF NEVADA. He was younger than the rest and his black hair was pomaded so that it shone like patent leather. He had a stiff white collar and the back of his neck was red with anger. Every once in a while he pounded his desk, and it seemed that every other sentence contained THE SOVEREIGN STATE OF NEVADA. Whenever he said this, his voice dropped and he pronounced each syllable as if he were talking about God. Pete had not taken the trouble to find out what his real name was. As far as Pete was concerned, the man's name was THE SOVEREIGN STATE OF NEVADA.

Pete recognized him as a new man. He recognized this because the man's desk was in the front row and he had a beaten-up old spittoon, and he talked too much. Pete had learned to distinguish between the new men and those who really counted.

There was an old man with a gray fringe of hair combed very carefully over his bald spot, and he was one of those who counted. His seat was in the very back row and he had a shiny new spittoon. From this, Pete knew that he had *seniority*. The old man was also not taking the trouble to listen to the new man's arguments, but had picked up a copy of the *Carson City Daily Appeal* and was reading it.

When the bill came to a vote, most of the heads in the chamber below turned furtively to peer back at the old man with the new spittoon. The old man set aside his newspaper, raised his hands to a little above desk level, and pointed his thumbs downward. When that happened, Pete knew, the Nos would very clearly outnumber the Ayes.

Pete sighed with deep satisfaction. And then he made the mistake of noticing that the back of the neck of THE SOVEREIGN STATE OF NEVADA had now turned purple. Pete could not smother his giggling. The face of THE SOVEREIGN STATE OF NEVADA turned upwards with both indignation and satisfaction written on it. Here at least was one encounter he could win. He leaped to his feet. "May I request the Speaker to instruct the Sergeant at Arms to kick that goddammed kid out of here so we can proceed with the business of THE SOVEREIGN STATE OF NEVADA?"

The Speaker's gavel descended and Pete was unceremoniously turned out into the snow and the cold.

15

The thin line of poplars that served the town as windbreak also marked the outer limits of the houses. The poplars' upward-thrusting branches had long since been blown clean of leaves, the sap had run back into their tapered trunks, and now they stood gray and dead with winter.

Lingering in their uncertain shelter, Pete knew a moment of uncertainty. Beyond the poplars was the unknown. Behind him was the certainty of home and shelter. When he had started out secretly from the little hotel, it had all seemed so simple. Now, he was not so sure. Then he remembered something that Miss Benton had quoted from a story they were reading in class: *To be afraid of a thing and yet to do it is what makes the prettiest kind of a man.*

Picturing the explorers who must have repeated the same words, Pete steeled himself and set out resolutely, deliberating which canyon he should choose. The wind began unexpectedly to rise, pouring out of the west and filling the bare branches with a soft roar. It flowed into his face, parting at his forehead and slipping past his cheekbones in a frozen stream.

Without a backward look at town, he chose his canyon and set out across the white expanse of fields that stretched from the line of poplars to where the deep forested mountains began. He felt secure in his Mackinaw jacket and boots and Lindy helmet, but he caught himself wishing he had worn his mittens, even though his friends said gloves were sissy. The left hand that held the hatchet was beginning to sting with cold. He remedied that by transferring the hatchet to his right hand and stuffing the other into the pocket of his Mackinaw until it could get warm again. In the deep pocket, his hand joined company with the bread and ham he had brought along as provisions. The book had said that was necessary for an expedition into the wilderness.

With frightening swiftness, the wind became stronger as though slow-moving nature had suddenly decided to show what it was capable of doing. White fragments of clouds led the storm, tearing over the white mountain peaks. The wind swept the light snow from the last storm off the pack that lay over the fields and whipped it into his face like slivers of ice. The eddies of the blown snow moved toward him like an invading army of wraiths.

As the explorers had, Pete bent his head to the storm and trudged onwards. For minutes at a time he was enveloped by drifting snow. He reveled in it. When he stopped to catch his breath, the world was over-whelmingly silent as if all sound had been caught between the softness underfoot and the softness overhead. The world became confined to a very little space around him, and he resented the times when the wind dropped and the veil of snow cleared to reveal patches of blue in the sky.

A thicket of willows loomed in the swirling white mist, and Pete de-cided to take refuge and eat some of his provisions. The mountains were upon him now and he would need his strength. Getting down on his knees, he burrowed into the willow thicket until he found a pocket that was protected from the wind. There were tiny, weightless tracks on the dusting of snow. Pete was delighted to find that sparrows had used this place as refuge, too. It meant that he had chosen wisely.

With the thick network of little branches surrounding him, it was almost like a cave. He brushed away the snow and the top leaves until he uncovered a layer that was only slightly wet, and hunkered down to eat. But when he tried opening the blade of his jack knife, he found that his fingers were getting numb. He gave it up and bit into the quarter loaf of bread and chewed the ham that had been cured with red pepper and admitted to himself that he was a damn fool for not bringing his mittens.

For the first time, he also caught himself wishing that he had asked one of his brothers to come with him. But having wished it, he put it out of his mind. The tree was to be his doing alone.

It wasn't that the family could not afford to buy a tree or that his father could not go cut one. It was just that neither his father nor his mother seemed to know that a Christmas tree went with Christmas, and the reason was tied up somehow with all the other unexplained things that came out of what they called "the old country."

Pete had considered telling them, but he had not been able to sum-mon up the courage. Whatever way it came out, it would have amounted to a reproach on his part and a failing on theirs. So, there was nothing else to do but keep quiet or tell a lie when his friends who lived in real houses instead of a hotel talked about their Christmas trees. Or worse yet, to have to walk past their homes on the back streets and see the dull glitter of Christmas trees trimmed with tinsel peeping through the windows and feel a pang of loss because Christmas in his family was not complete.

Chewing on the ham that burned the roof of his mouth, Pete reflected that the business of a tree meant more to him than Santa Claus. He had lost his illusions about Santa Claus at a very early age. It happened one night after the American Legion Christmas party for all the kids in town, when they had trooped up dutifully to accept their presents from that terrifying apparition in a red costume and a long white beard.

When the American Legion party was done, he and his brothers and sisters had gone straight to the kitchen of the little hotel to open their presents. The front door of the hotel burst open and Santa Claus came shuffling down the long dining room jingling the sleigh bells he carried over one shoulder. They had all scurried for cover to their common bedroom and locked the door.

Santa Claus did not pursue them, but they could hear his hearty laugh and the jingling of the bells from the kitchen. Pete had tiptoed to the door and opened it a crack just in time to see Santa Claus hoisting a shot glass of whiskey to his lips. The revelation that Santa Claus drank whiskey did not bother Pete, but the way in which his lips curled around the shot glass did. There was only one man who drank his whiskey that way. The menace of the apparition dissolved and Pete knew that Santa Claus was only the old prospector, Mickey McCluskey, got up in costume.

Scattering the remains of his bread and ham on the dusting of snow around him for the sparrows to eat, Pete crawled stiffly out of his willow cave. When he stood up, his heart gave a little jump of fear. The wind had died, but it had done its work of bringing in the storm. The air was so filled with huge snowflakes that he could barely make out the evergreens on the white mountain above him. He took a backward look across the fields to town, but the town was no longer to be seen. His chest tightened with a spasm of terror, and he very nearly abandoned his quest. But when he faced the mountain again, the stubborn streak in him took hold. He had come too far to give up now.

Again, Pete bent his head to the storm, but this time it had nothing to do with pretending he was an explorer. There was a Christmas tree to be cut, and in a hurry, before the snow got too deep. It was already around his waist, and the higher he climbed, the deeper it got.

Without being aware of it, he was following the firm backbone of a ridge that led into the mountains. He had no way of knowing that the inviting smoothness of the ravine below meant really deep snow that concealed many things. But it was in the ravine that he saw what he had come in search of. Through the fragmented curtain of falling snow, he made out the form of a perfect Christmas tree of feathered fir almost hidden in a grove of giant pines, and he went down into the ravine. In one hopeless instant of realization, he knew he had made a mistake. He stepped off solid footing into nothing.

He screamed one lost scream as the snow enveloped him and closed over his head. He began flailing to beat the suffocating substance of it from his nose and mouth. His fall ended, but he did not pay any attention to that. To his astonishment, he found that he could breathe. He cowered in the white darkness, coughing out the snow that had gotten into his throat and gulping lungfuls of air. When he was breathing regularly again, the terror began to ebb and he saw that his hands had beaten out a pocket in front of his face. He stood without daring to move and so disturb that fragile space of air that meant breath and life. The snow that had burned his nostrils and his lungs had also given him his first smell of death.

It was a long time before he felt the trickle of melting snow running down inside his collar and across his back. When it washed its way into his consciousness, he realized that he had been staring without comprehension at a patch of bare earth showing through the wall of snow in front of him. His eyes clung to the presence of dirt as if it were the only permanent thing in life.

He was thinking more clearly now. The dirt meant that he had fallen into a hole, and he tried to recall how far he had fallen. He remembered that it had not been far at all, and for an instant, he was reassured. Then the thought struck him that he may be upside down, and the terror returned and he began to sob. He surrendered to the crying until he could cry no more, and then his mind was clear again. Now, he knew that his fall had been a sliding one and that he had not rolled.

Tentatively, he moved his hand out to scrape the snow from around the patch of earth. His fingertips told him two things. The ground sloped out gradually, so he had to be standing right side up. Also, it was scarred with the deep grooves that a miner's pick makes. The feel of the grooves was familiar to him. In the other mountains, the desert mountains to the east of town, he and Tony had climbed into enough prospectors' holes scarred with the same kind of grooves.

All it would take to get out would be one sustained scramble. Unless he slipped. At the prospect of that, his courage faltered. He closed his eyes and heard himself reciting a Hail Mary. It was not a very good one, because the voice he heard was a whimper. He recited another and then another and heard his voice grow stronger.

When he opened his eyes again, he knew there was no choice for him. It was either stay in the hole and die without trying, or die trying to get out. Bringing his legs together slowly, he took in as much air as his lungs could hold, and lunged for the side of the hole. With hands and feet clawing at the earth behind the snow, he propelled himself upwards. He did not slip, but his lungs could not hold breath any longer. His mouth gaped open and the snow came in, and then in the next instant, his head had burst through into the air.

Vomiting the snow out of his throat, he went down on all fours and dug his way like a burrowing animal to the blurred outline of a pine with low hanging limbs. When he gained it, he reached up and his hands closed over the rough bark of an unyielding branch. He clung to the branch like a man drowning.

After a while, the trembling stopped and he realized that the snow on which his feet trailed was firm. He let himself down easily and stood upright. In disbelief, he shifted his weight from one foot to the other to feel the solidity beneath him. When he raised his eyes, he saw the ridge above him and the tracks he had made coming down into the ravine. The tracks were filling with new snow, but suddenly, the fact that it was snowing was a matter of no consequence. He had escaped from the hole that had almost been his grave, and he was alive. All that was needed now was to follow his own tracks home.

And then, two things met his eyes almost at the same instant. One was the brown wood handle of the hatchet peeping like a traitor out of the snow where it had been flung when he began to fall, and directly in front of him, the feathered little tree he had come down to cut. He stared at the tree in despair. All he wanted was to be free of his obligation and go home to warmth. But there was no escaping. He had come too far to go home empty handed. With bitterness in his heart, he picked up the hatchet and plowed his way to the tree and cut it down.

Afterwards, he could not remember much of the long trip home, except that the boughs of the tree on his shoulder kept obscuring his vision and that he fell less often when he had descended from the mountain and gained the even ground of the fields.

He had planned to rest when he reached the safety of the thin line of poplars on the edge of town, but it did not seem worthwhile. By then, he had lost sensation in the hand that held the hatchet, he could not feel the tree trunk biting into his shoulder anymore, and home was only a few blocks away. The lights had come on in the houses on the back streets, and snowflakes played in the glow from the streetlamps overhead. Muffled by closed doors and made soft by falling snow, the high clear voices of children singing carols reached out from a big house.

Main Street was deserted when he reached it. The storm had driven everyone inside. The only lights on his block came from the Columbo and, beyond that, the little hotel. He paused in front of the hotel, trying to straighten himself for the triumphant entry he had daydreamed about sometime in the hazed past. But to straighten up was impossible, so he merely pushed open the door and went inside. Light and warmth and the voices of his sisters, changing in an instant from tears to delight, flooded over him. And then something happened. It was as if the thin wire that had sustained him snapped like a violin string. The tree rolled from his shoulder and the hatchet fell from his hand.

Faces swam into his vision, were transfixed, and then slipped away. He saw his father's face and his eyes wild with worry, Mizoo's long face framed by the collar of a heavy coat, the sheriff's fat face in a furry cap and earmuffs and his saying something about a search party, and his mother's face with eyes bigger and darker than he had ever seen and her mouth framing a question.

Pete heard his own voice. It came out in croaking he did not recognize. "It's a Christmas tree."

He tried to take a step. His father caught him when he fell. Pete felt the strong arms close around him and pick him up like a child. And because nothing further was required on his part, Pete leaned his face against his father's chest and went to sleep.

16

Without lifting his head from the pillow, Pete gazed with vague wonderment at the lace curtains that covered the bedroom window. They were new, but it seemed that he had been awakening to them for a long time and that always before, they had been dead and still. Now, they were actually trembling. That was unusual enough, but the morning breeze that came in through the crack actually carried with it the smell of first growing things.

He sighed with satisfaction, knowing that spring had finally come. He knew other things, too. He knew that the wind had turned to the south and had dried up every last bit of snow, except maybe the patch that always stayed the longest, because it lay on the north side of the shed in the back yard and the wind always had trouble creeping around there.

He knew also that in a few minutes, when he had come fully awake, he could walk out into the soft air and see the fragile blue sky of spring and the ground newly come up out of the snow. The ground would be black and moist and the rich smell of it would rise up and fill him to brimming. And he would have on his tennis shoes, because after the long winter, that kind of ground made him want to run and run and run until he dropped. While he was running, an unexpected puff of cold wind would come from the snow-covered mountains to the west, and he could laugh with satisfaction because it was still winter up there and spring down here.

But where had winter gone? He could not remember its passing. Its presence had been as fleeting as the figures that had tiptoed through the darkened room like shadows in a dream. He came wide awake then, wrestling with the huge question of where winter had gone. The last thing he could remember clearly was Christmas and the tinseled tree in the long dining room. There had been presents, and he had gotten a cap pistol and a football cobbled with the grain of pigskin and giving off the smell of new leather. Then he remembered that one day his throat had begun to burn and that his legs were hurting. And one night he had sat smack down on the kitchen floor because his legs had hurt too much to support him.

A partition in the bedroom had materialized from somewhere, separating him from his brothers and sisters, and the lights had gotten dim and stayed that way in the days and nights. The doctor had come for the first of many shadowy visits, to place a piece of cold metal on his chest and listen to his heart through rubber tubes. And in the nights, the door had cracked and he had pretended to be asleep when his mother came in on slippered feet, and her hand had crept in under the covers and rested on his chest in the same place as the doctor's cold piece of metal, feeling for his life.

There had been visitors in the days, too. His brothers and sisters came to stand at the head of the bed and stare at him as if he were a stranger, and once his father had sat down on the edge of the bed and rested his huge hand on Pete's as if to pass his strength to him. And Pete had looked away with eyes brimming with tears that he no longer had the strength to fight back.

He remembered Mizoo tiptoeing in with his big ten-gallon hat in his hands and Mickey McCluskey mumbling something intended to be cheerful while his breath filled the room with the smell of whiskey and his eyes glistened in the dim light. And then one time Pete had awakened to the smell of incense and oil and burning tapers and the priest intoning words in Latin over him. And after that, Pete had had nightmares that he had died, after all, crouched in a white grave with a great weight of snow bearing down upon him.

But all that seemed to have happened a long time ago, before this morning and the cool breeze that washed through the partly open window with the first smell of spring. Something must have happened in the night to make the half life he had been living go away.

Very tentatively, he moved his legs under the covers. There was no pain. He considered this remarkable development with distrust. The pain was only hiding for a moment before leaping out to seize him. He lay still, waiting, but no pain came. Perhaps it really was gone, at least from his legs, and he wondered how it was with his arms. He waited a while longer and then he raised his right arm until it was high enough off the coverlet to come into his vision. The sight that met his eyes made him recoil with disgust. Protruding from the sleeve of his nightgown was a white stick of an arm with an obscene knob for an elbow.

And then Pete remembered what had been eluding him. It was the voice of the doctor carrying through the closed door of his bedroom.

The doctor had said in a murmur made rough by need, "I am not going to hold out false hopes to you. The rheumatic fever has ruined his heart. He will never be the boy he was before. He will not be able to play at sports with the other boys because he cannot be allowed to run. And if he lives that long, he will be only half a man."

Now, finally, Pete understood what the words meant. He let the thing that was his arm drop to the coverlet. And then he turned his head away so that he would not have to look at the trembling curtains and the square of light that had betrayed him, because they told of spring and black moist earth and the time for tennis shoes and running until he could run no more.

17

Later, Pete was to reflect that if it had not been for his having to be confined to bed, he would never have discovered his brothers and sisters. Before, he could not remember knowing much about them except their names. He had taken their presence for granted because they had always been around.

The only exception was the time his mother had surprisingly taken to her bed, and Mae Murphy, who was something called a midwife, had come to the hotel. She had ordered him and his brothers and sister out of their bedroom and told them to go play outside because their mother was sick. Out of whatever the sickness was had come his little sister, Michelle. Pete had gone in dutifully to look at the baby and dismissed her immediately as being too small to be of any importance. And in a few days, his mother was up and about and back to her cooking as if nothing had happened.

It took Pete a while to suspect that it was his mother who made the family come in to keep him company. One day, he had been sat up in bed with pillows to prop him. His mother had laid his pipestem arms and thin white hands on the coverlet, but as soon as she was gone, he put his hands under the covers so that he would not have to look at them.

His sisters came in almost on tiptoe and sat down on either side of his bed, their hands folded in their laps, and stared at him without saying a word. Though it was a Saturday, they were dressed in their school clothes, with starched dresses that made a rustling sound when they moved and with their hair done up in ringlets. He shifted uncomfortably under their gaze. It was as if they were looking at something that was not quite human.

The older of them, Suzette, sat very straight and silent, looking at him out of her gray eyes and turning away once in a while to regard her hands. She had a long face and slightly protruding teeth. When Pete had had his mean times, he had made fun of her teeth. Now, in repose, he saw that she was sort of pretty at that with her auburn hair and gray-flecked eyes and a wide mouth like their father's.

And then Pete noticed for the first time that his little sister, Michelle, had the same gray eyes, except that when she smiled as she was doing now, her eyes crinkled shut.

"Do you want to play jacks, Pete?" said Michelle, plunging her hand in her pocket and coming up with jacks and a red rubber ball.

Suzette drew herself up even straighter. "I knew you were going to sneak those jacks in here. You know what Mama said!"

Michelle returned the jacks to her pocket, but her chin thrust out belligerently. "I don't see why not. It's only a girls' game and Pete's a boy, so it won't hurt him."

"What did Mama say?" Pete asked.

"She said we weren't supposed to excite you," said Suzette.

"Why not?" Pete asked.

Suzette would not answer. She knew she had said too much already. But Michelle said blithely, "Because it might make your heart stop and then you would be dead."

The tears had been coming easily for a long time now, and nothing Pete could do seemed to prevent them. They rolled down his cheeks and he felt sick with revulsion at what he had become.

Suzette leaped to her feet. "See what I told you!" she said to Michelle.

At the aspect of his crying, Michelle turned pale and began to whimper with a fear she did not understand. That was enough to make Pete stop crying and come to her defense. He took his hands out from under the covers and held them out to Michelle. "Come on. You can teach me how to play jacks."

It occurred to Pete while they were playing that he would never have been caught dead playing a girls' game before. But now he did not care about that, or anything else for that matter. It was simply another humiliation heaped on him, like his father having to carry him to the bathroom and watch over him so that he did not fall. The expression in his sisters' eyes when they had come in had not lied. He had become something that was not quite human.

But he became confused again when his brothers came in their turn. His little brothers Mike and Gene sprawled unconcernedly on the bottom of the bed. Gene picked up a funny book and began to read it, and little Mike, still roly poly with baby fat, rested his chin on his hand and said, "Do you hurt anymore, Pete? How does it feel when it hurts?"

Pete tried to answer but did not know how to explain it. His big brother, Leon, was standing beside the bed looking down at him. "The doctor says the hurt is gone," he said, "so there's no sense asking about it. You can't remember pain."

Pete looked up at him. "That's right. I just can't remember it."

"Well, you shouldn't think about it, anyway," said Leon, "because it's over and done with. Now you got to get some meat on your bones." He added a thought he had copycatted from the Senator's speech: "Never look back." Leon was learning quickly, Pete realized.

"Aw," said Gene without looking up from his funny book. "Mama says he's going to be an invalid." He pronounced the word as if he were not quite sure of the syllables.

"What's an invalid?" said Mike, his forehead puckering.

Pete could tell that Leon wasn't quite sure, but he bluffed it out anyway. "You're too little to understand. There's no sense me explaining it to you until you grow up." He changed the subject in a hurry. "Wanna play some checkers, Pete?"

"I get to play the winner," said Gene a second before Mike.

And so Pete quit staring at the wall and lived for the times when he could play jacks with his sisters and checkers with his brothers. He also began trying not to listen to the shouts and laughter that came in through the open window, from where his brothers and their friends played outside in the warmth of a sun that Pete could scarcely remember.

18

Mizoo's ten-gallon hat was tipped back on his head and his cowboy boots, which were really laced boots with a built-up heel, were tucked under the chair in Pete's improvised bedroom.

"There was the time this dude come to town," Mizoo drawled. "He was making quite a show about that he wanted to buy a good hoss. He tried out a passel of 'em, but they was none good enough, it seemed like. So I said to him, 'Let's go down to the river ranch. There's a dago down there who's got high-blood hosses.' So we goes down to the river ranch, and looks over them hosses. Right away, he spots a gelding that was a pretty thing at that, I'll tell you. So the dude says to the dago, 'I do want that animal.' The dago says, 'I no want to sella him. He no lookee good.'"

Mizoo paused to shift the quid of tobacco from one side of his long face to the other. "But the dude," he said, his eyes squinting mischievously, "wouldn't take no for an answer, and he commands the dago to saddle him up. The dago shakes his head but does what the man wants. Well, that there dude gets on that hoss and puts them fancy English spurs to him proper. Fust thing that hoss does is run right into a fence, from which he caroms off like a pool ball and proceeds to run smack into the river. The dude crawls out soppin' wet and says to the dago, 'Why didn't you tell me he was blind?' And the dago says, 'I try to tell you! He no lookee good.'"

When it came time for Buckshot to visit, Pete saw with astonishment that he had actually shaved off his black stubble of beard for the occasion.

"Now, you got to understand that not one of the three of us had been ten miles from Carson City in our lives," said Buckshot. "So you can see how easy it was for us to get lost at something like a world's fair, in a city like San Francisco. Well, sure enough, we got separated on the second day. We just plain out lost poor Matt Farrell in the crowd. Pickles and me, we hunted high and low, but Matt Farrell was nowhere to be found. We were getting kind of desperate. Then Pickles comes up with the answer of how to find Matt, just like that. So we do it. We go back to the ticket taker at the entrance to the world's fair in San Francisco and we ask him, 'Have you seen Matt Farrell lately?' That ticket taker, he looks at us sort of funny at first, and then he says, 'Nope. I haven't seen good old Matt for three hours at least.' Now, can you imagine that, Pete? All those thousands of people that ticket taker saw that day, and he could still remember the last time he saw Matt Farrell!"

·

Mickey McCluskey had not gone without his ration of whiskey this day, Pete could tell from his breath. If anything, he had trebled it, to the point that his eyes were swimming.

"Well, as I was standing there making a purchase of side bacon for my prospecting trip to the Amargosa desert, where as ye know the jackass rabbits are obliged to carry canteens," said Mickey McCluskey, "who should come in but that big buck Injun Captain Tom who as ye well know has a failing for cheese. My business being completed, I decides to wait and watch the proceedings. 'I want um cheese,' says Captain Tom to Sam the butcher, as if Sam didn't know that. In fact, Sam the butcher already has the cheese laying on the counter and his knife at the ready. 'How much?' Sam the butcher says to Captain Tom. 'Ten cents,' says Captain Tom, producing the most worn out dime ye ever saw. Well, Sam the butcher slides his big knife down carefully and cuts Captain Tom a slice. Captain Tom, his face don't twitch a muscle but he leans down to take a close look. 'Umm!' says he. 'You almost miss um.'"

·

"I was thinking we could read the newspaper together," said Pansy Gifford in his breathless child's voice, producing that afternoon's *Carson City Daily Appeal* fresh from Bergen's pool hall. He was a handyman around town who tried to conceal his station by wearing a suit and a tie, and from spring through autumn a pansy in his lapel, even when he was doing the meanest of jobs. When he walked down the street, he carried a folded newspaper so that he could point to it while he was discussing the day's happenings with other people who wore suits, too. Pansy sat down in the straight chair beside Pete's bed and fumbled in his coat pocket and said, as always, "I seem to have forgotten my glasses. Would you be a good boy and read the news of the day to me?" And as Pete read, Pansy leaned closer and said, as always, "Where exactly does it say that?" And once, Pansy shook his head and said sadly, "You know, Pete, there's people who died this year that never died before. It seems like everybody I know is either alive or dead." When Pete was done,

Pansy took the newspaper and folded it carefully under his arm and said, "Well, I got to go now. It's time to irrigate the water." He paused at the door and waved with his fingers like a little boy. "Goodbye, Pete. I'll see you tomorrow, same time." He paused when he was through the door and stuck his head back and said brightly, "Let's hope the news of the day will be better."

.

And then there was Hallelujah Bob in his stovepipe hat and handlebar moustaches, who came in under the watchful eye of his mother.

Hallelujah Bob was something called a *remittance man,* which meant that he was sent money every month by his family in Switzerland if he promised not to come back home and embarrass them anymore. Hallelujah Bob had his own ideas about why Pete was sick, and those ideas did not agree with the doctor's.

Hallelujah Bob was convinced that Pete was haunted by evil spirits, and there was a certain cure for that. Pete already knew what the cure was. Every time Hallelujah Bob got drunk and the spirits inside him brought on the presence of spirits outside, he simply blasted away at them with his shotgun, yelling out with every shot, "Hallelujah! I got one that time!"

Hallelujah Bob's shack had the reputation of being the best ventilated house in town.

.

Joe Wabuska had biting blue eyes in a bronzed face that showed the Indian blood people said his family carried.

"People have got it fixed in their minds that I've got a bum heart from the same thing you have now," he said with remembered heat in his eyes. "They don't know what they're talking about. I've proved it to them a hundred times, and I will have to go on proving it until I've beat the hell out of every son of a bitch in this town. I'll tell you a secret, Pete. If you listen to that doctor, you are going to be an invalid for the rest of your life. But if you make up your mind to get out of that bed, you'll be able to do anything anybody else can do. Here, these are for you. You'll grow into them in time. I'm making a bet you will grow up to be the horseback rider your father is." Joe Wabuska laid a pair of cowboy boots on Pete's bed. They were fronted with hand engraved designs and had soft leather insides that were creamy white with newness. Something kept intruding itself into Pete's thoughts. His fingers following the design grooves, he suddenly remembered what it was. In his mother's metal box, there was a blurred photograph of a man on a big horse. The man had a long black scarf wrapped around his neck, a leather vest, studded gauntlets on his arms, and high black cowboy boots. And the man was his father.

19

It was a morning when his brothers and sisters had gone to school and the little hotel was quiet. With the sunlight streaming through the window, his mother and he sat surrounded by the contents of the metal box.

It had begun when he had asked to see the photograph of his father on a horse. Pete had studied it intently and saw that it really was his father, after all. But so different, not only in what Pete was used to seeing him wearing, but in the expression on his face and the sure way he sat on his horse with an elbow thrust out and the doubled-up fist rammed against his waist. Pete had said, "He looks dangerous." And his mother had said, "If you mean he's got a bad temper, yes."

The other pictures were mystifying, too. They were of sheep spread out in the desert as far as his eye could see, of corrals filled with cattle, of buckaroos in beaten-up hats and worn shirts who were so unlike the cowboys in the movies that Pete decided they must have been poor cowboys, of sheepherders with shaggy dogs at their feet who looked even poorer.

"Was Papa a cowboy?" he asked.

"No," she said. "I mean he had cows, but mostly it was the sheep."

Pete was disappointed. "Then why did he ride a horse?"

"Well, sheepmen ride horses, too," she said. "How else are they going to get around out there where there's no roads?"

They went hurriedly then through what she said were pictures from the Basque country of France. Too hurriedly, Pete thought later, but he was not that much interested in them, anyway. His mother paused once, however, to look at one picture longer than the others. It was of two girls, one standing and the other sitting down in a fancy chair.

Pete held out his hand for the picture. "Who are they?"

"My sisters," she said.

"Then I have aunts like other kids?"

"Of course."

The idea of relatives in a foreign land was new to Pete. It was something he would have to think about later. "Do I have a grandmother?"

"No," his mother said. "She died before I came to this country."

"Is my grandfather dead, too?"

His mother nodded fiercely and began gathering up the old-country pictures. As though to turn his attention away, she handed him one last picture. It was of a large white house surrounded by trees. "That was our house."

"In France?"

"Of course not," she said. "That was our ranch house when you were a baby."

Pete stared at the picture with astonishment. "You mean I lived in that house."

She regarded him as he held the picture close to inspect every detail of the house, and her brow knitted. "Would you like to live in a house?"

"Who wouldn't!"

His mother turned her head away as if struck with a thought. "Hmmm," she said, and then made the sound again. Absent-mindedly, as though she had forgotten his presence, she closed the metal box and left the room.

20

Because it was laced with fear, Pete thought he was having a nightmare. There had been voices raised in anger and his father's voice with an iron edge running through it, and in counterpoint the whimpering of his little sister, Michelle, and the shushing tones of Suzette, and every once in a while, the shuffling of bare feet and the urgent whispering of Leon.

When he realized that it was no nightmare at all, Pete came awake with eyes wide open, his heart thudding against his chest. Something frightful was happening in the kitchen and it had to do with his mother and father. He lay stiff with terror as the disembodied voices came through the wall.

"We know for an absolute fact that you are serving alcoholic spirits in this establishment," the authoritative voice said. It was the Prohi agent with the bitter mouth and wire-rimmed glasses, and Pete felt his heart jump and almost falter at the recognition of it.

"You can't prove that," his father said, his voice breaking with the effort of restraint.

"We are going to prove it by searching this establishment," the Prohi agent said.

His father's voice was deadly now. "No! You are not going to search anything."

"I warn you . . ." the Prohi agent began, but the words were drowned by the hysterical pleading of his mother. "Please! We have a sick child back there."

The Prohi's voice lowered in false politeness. "Lady, we're not going to search your sick child. We are going to search the premises, whether you like it or not."

His father's voice lost all restraint now. "You can't talk to my wife like that."

The Prohi's voice was contemptuous. "I'll talk to bootleggers any way I please."

The harsh burst of rushing footsteps came through the wall, and then a scream of pain. Pete smelled the unaccountable smell of burning wool. From the bedroom next to his, Pete heard Leon's horrified whisper, "Oh, my God! Papa picked him up and set him on the stove." And then, Leon's voice again, but this time it was heavy with fright. "Oh, my God! The Prohi's pulled a gun."

"I ought to shoot you right here!" the Prohi cried in mingled pain and rage. But there was something else in his voice, too.

"Do you think that gun scares *me*?" his father shouted. And again, there was the sound of rushing feet. But this time, it was not only one set of footsteps, but three, and they echoed and then diminished and then were gone.

Pete heard a great sigh from Leon. "By God! He ran 'em out."

The front door of the hotel slammed shut with a bang, and then his father's footsteps sounded, returning to the kitchen. "That does it! I've got to get out of this place before I kill one of them."

His mother's voice was normal now, and there was determination in it. "Not only you," she said.

His mother and his father talked in hushed tones and Pete could not hear what they were saying. After a while, he heard his mother come into the back part of the hotel and tiptoe into his bedroom. He closed his eyes and pretended to be asleep. His mother's hand crept under the covers and came to rest over his heart. He opened his eyes and said, "I'm all right, Mama."

"Did you hear?" she said.

"Did Papa really set him down on the hot stove?" said Pete.

His mother stiffened. "It wasn't funny," she said, and covered her face with her hands. "I'm ashamed you had to hear it."

P · A · R · T   T · W · O

S · U · M · M · E · R

1

Shadows of leaves moved in rhythmic patterns across the pages of the book lying open in his lap. The leaves had jagged edges and they moved first in one direction across the pages and then returned to where they began. Their movement was hypnotic and Pete forgot what he was reading as he watched them.

The screened porch in which he sat was shielded from the prying eyes of neighbors by growths of ivy that grew up thickly on all three sides. The whir of the lawnmower his brother Leon was pushing was more distant now. He had finished with the stretch of lawn that lay between the porch and the high hedge in front of the house, and was working his way around the trunks of the poplars that lined the street on the other side of the walk. From time to time, his close-cropped head and sunburned face rose above the high hedge and then dipped and disappeared.

Somewhere in the immensity of the house behind Pete, his sisters were playing in their bedroom and his mother was sitting in the sunny alcove that jutted out from the living room, embroidering doilies for the marble-topped tables that seemed to stand in every one of a hundred corners.

The house, bought with money his parents had made from selling the hotel, was not nearly so intimidating now as it was when they had first moved in. Pete had been awed by its size, and he had also been frightened. After the confinement of the little rooms into which they had been packed in the back of the hotel, the house had seemed altogether too big for safety. Since he had just begun to take a few tentative steps, Pete had come into the house from the vantage point of a perch on his father's shoulder.

They had passed through the hedge and seen walkways and flower beds and even a lawn that was their very own. He had liked the screened-in porch immediately because of its combination of fresh air and protection. The foyer beyond the heavy front door and its oval of glass was another matter. Though it was only an entrance room, it was as big as all their bedrooms combined in the hotel. It was filled with doors that went in every direction, all closed and all holding secrets.

The living room had taken his breath away with its splendor. There was a chandelier hanging from a high ceiling, and carpet on the floor, and huge leather armchairs and sofas and a monstrous grand piano of dark, burnished wood. The biggest doors he had ever seen outside of the capitol opened into the dining room with a gleaming table and a buffet filled clear to its top with glasses and china.

He remembered their first supper at the dining room table. It had been too quiet, with none of the familiar crash of pots and pans and plates, the clumping of Mizoo's boots on the wooden floor, and ten conversations going on at the same time between prospectors and buckaroos and sheepherders and working men and bachelor politicians with high white collars and big stomachs crossed by watch chains. His father had been the most ill at ease, putting his elbows on the table and taking them off again. Pete was not far behind him, but his brother Leon, like their mother, had been right at home from the start. Leon acted as if he had been born to the house and all its elegance. Pete had tried to emulate him and it had helped finally. But there were still nights in which he cried out in terror from unfamiliar creakings that brought on nightmares of unexplained presences in the vastness of the house. His mother had quieted his fears, setting them down to his sickness, but that had not helped much at all. What helped most was the mornings when sunlight filtered through the windows and cool peace pervaded the house.

But though the house was not nearly so intimidating now, the neighborhood still was. They had moved only six blocks away from the little hotel, but it might as well have been six hundred miles. This was what was known as the respectable part of Carson City, with tree-shaded streets and blocks filled with houses, some even bigger than this one. Dressed-up men and women in neckties and panama hats and sunbonnets and gauzy dresses strolled on neat sidewalks on summer afternoons and in the evenings. High-toned people, as his father called them, lived in these houses. People like judges and lawyers and doctors and politicians. The Governor's mansion lay only a few blocks away in all its white-pillared magnificence.

Pete secretly hated the high-toned people. He hated them because in the two months since his family had moved into the neighborhood, not one of them had come to visit. From the protection of the screened porch, Pete had watched them pass by in their strolling. And he had heard them murmuring to each other, thinking they were not overheard.

He had caught the words, *foreigners of some sort. Basque, I think, whatever that is,* and another time, the epithet he hated most in the world.

Peeping through the thickly clinging ivy, he leaned forward now to watch two of them go by. The woman was like the rest of them, haughty in her sunbonnet and delicate glasses that hung from a brooch on her fancy dress. The man was dressed up, too, but Pete had to admit he did not carry himself like his wife.

The whir of the lawnmower stopped, and to his amazement, Pete heard Leon's voice. He was actually talking to the high-toned people, or at least to the man.

"You're doing a good piece of work there, son," the man said.

"It's sort of fun," said Leon.

"That's because you're young," the man said. There was a pause as if he were thinking something over, and then he said, "Would you like to cut our lawn? I'll pay you."

"All right," said Leon in a voice gone suddenly responsible.

The man told Leon where he lived and they set a time for the next day. He nodded goodbye and then he and his stuck-up wife went on down the sidewalk. With fury rising inside him, Pete went back to his rocking chair and picked up the book and pretended to read. But he could not contain himself. When Leon had finished his mowing and come into the porch to flop out on the hammock hanging from the ceiling, Pete confronted him. "Why did you say you'd cut their lawn?"

"Why not?" Leon said without looking up. "It means money and I'm broke."

"But for *them*?" Pete cried. "She didn't even speak to you. Not one word!"

Leon raised himself on an elbow and regarded Pete with puzzlement. Then he divined the cause of Pete's anger. "Aw," he said easily. "They're people like anybody else. Give 'em a chance. They'll get used to us."

Leon flopped down again on the hammock and was instantly hidden from view. Pete stared at the hammock with incredulity. His brother had betrayed him. Suddenly, he felt desperately lonely for the company of Mizoo and Mickey McCluskey and Buckshot and even Wash. He wondered if he would ever see them again and decided certainly not here in this fancy house.

Leon was asleep and snoring lightly. Setting down his book, Pete got to his feet and walked unsteadily to the porch door. He opened it quietly. The high hedge seemed far away, but he took his time until he had passed through the gate and made good his escape. The long, shaded sidewalk stretched out interminably in front of him, and he almost turned back. Then he remembered how before, it would have taken him five seconds to run that distance. The thought propelled him down the length of the sidewalk and the next one and then to the street that in time would lead him to downtown and the little hotel. When he turned the corner and began walking down the middle of the street, he saw that someone was watching him. It was the man who was going to pay Leon for cutting the lawn. The man's figure was at times indistinct, but Pete saw that he was not dressed up any longer. He was in his shirtsleeves and he was watering his lawn. He was also watching Pete curiously.

Pete ducked his head and hurried his footsteps. It was becoming harder to breathe and he wished the sun were not so terribly hot. Stopping for a moment, he saw a white picket fence and crossed to the sidewalk to lean against it until he could get his breath. When he realized that he would not be able to make it to the main street, he turned slowly to retrace his steps. Something was happening to his vision. The street and the houses and the treetops had begun to whirl in front of his eyes, and somewhere through the maze of moving objects, he saw a flopping hose and the figure of the man in his shirtsleeves running toward him. Then the sidewalk came up and he felt its jarring impact and then nothing.

When he awoke, it was to feel the familiar cold steel of the doctor's stethoscope against his heart, the ends of it sticking into the doctor's hairy ears. The room was cool and quiet, not at all like the room where all this had happened before. But the faces that surrounded him were the same, with one exception. Unexplainably, it was that of the high-toned man. Pete saw that the man was in his shirtsleeves, and then he remembered everything.

The cold disc left his chest and the doctor said, "He's all right, but it was a close one." The doctor buttoned Pete's shirt and said, "Where in the devil were you going, son?"

Pete turned his head away. "Home."

There was a moment of perplexed silence, and then Pete heard Leon's exasperated voice. "I just don't understand you, Pete. I don't understand you at all!"

2

Their life had changed in more ways than the fact of a house and a strange neighborhood. It had to do with their father.

He had lingered in the alien setting only long enough to make sure the family was firmly installed, and then he was gone as if he were fleeing from something. In the beginning, it was from early morning until night, but as time went by he would be absent for days on end.

Once, he came back home with a big Dodge truck equipped with stock racks for animals, and the old Nash with the chrome headlights was relegated to the cavernous barn in the back yard, there to remain until it was hauled away for junk. The barn began to fill up with a weird assortment of things. There were canvas tents, saddles and packbags, sheep hooks, sacks of stock salt, wooden packsaddles for donkeys, bed-rolls, coal-oil lanterns, fire irons, and branding irons. And not all of them were newly bought. Things like hair chaps and carbines and a long, ominous pistol with a cartridge belt were beaten and scarred from long use. It seemed that their Uncle Joanes, who was a cattleman, had been storing them during all the years the family was in the little hotel.

Uncle Joanes with his coarse black hair and the same long chiseled face looked like their father, but he was shorter by far. In the family's time in the hotel, Pete had seen him only in fleeting moments. Pete had not paid much attention to him then, but now he learned that this wiry, hard little man had a wealth of stories to tell, like the one about the time during the range wars when he had his horse shot out from under him and had fought off two cowboys until dark with that same scarred carbine. Pete was never quite sure how many of the stories were true. They sounded suspiciously like Mizoo's.

Listening to his uncle and his father, Pete was learning words and expressions he had never heard before. This was the second time he had had to learn a new vocabulary. The first was when the family had moved into the house, and Pete had not known even what *living room* meant. Now, it seemed that his father and Uncle Joanes were *going in* together to *run sheep,* Uncle Joanes having *sold off* his cattle because beef prices were bad.

The reason for his father's absences also became clear. He was busy buying *breeding ewes* and arranging for forest service permits to graze on the *public domain,* and negotiating for *private parcels* of land in be-tween. Pete gathered that Uncle Joanes would be herding the sheep and his father would *handle the business end,* rebuild the corrals and *lambing pens* at the abandoned ranch they had leased in the *winter desert range,* and also be the camptender, which meant buying provisions for Uncle Joanes and taking them to him in the mountains by truck or horseback.

How their father had changed! Gone were the necktie and the suit pants and town shoes, and in their place were Levi's and a workshirt, boots and Stetson. Gone also were the murderous flares of temper and the caged expression and the white skin that came from working inside. Now, he was bronzed by the sun, his hands were hardened and nicked by barbed wire and slivers, and his spirit was lighthearted as a boy's. He laughed and told rough jokes and teased Suzette and Michelle until they were convulsed and crimson with laughter.

But as their father had changed, so had their mother. At first, she was content and tranquil with the new life and the time to embroider and sew and care for the household. Then, her mood changed to one of resentment at his prolonged absences, worry about the future, and finally a firm-jawed assuming of responsibility for her children. It had happened slowly and in subtle ways, but in the end, control of the house and family shifted to her hands. None of them could leave the house without telling her where they were going, how long they would be gone, exactly what hour they would be back, and whom they were going to be with. This last was the most important of all. She talked of the evils of bad company and intoned proverbs like, *Tell me who your friends are, and I will tell you who you are.*

The only one excepted from household rules was Leon. Because he was the eldest son, and also because he could be counted upon not to get into trouble, their mother began drawing him aside for private talks about such things as business and the welfare of the family.

Her resentment and her worries finally surfaced one night when their father came home just in time for supper. He was in good humor, and seemed to Pete like a black-haired giant whose ruddy strength was too big for the room. It began when Pete asked when he could come and see the sheep, and by the way to try out his boots on one of his father's horses.

"How do you feel?" his father said.

"I'm fine, Papa," said Pete. "I can walk pretty near anywhere now."

"Well, you got some time before school starts, ain't you?" his father said. "I think it would do you good."

His mother had overheard the conversation on her way in from the kitchen. She placed the steaming bowl of stew on the dining room table, and Pete saw that her hands were shaking. "No!" she said, her eyes blazing with an indignation that shook Pete to the core. "He's not going out with those sheep. Now or ever!"

The good humor began to fade from his father's face. "What's wrong with the sheep?"

"You know what's wrong with the sheep," she said. "They ruined us before and they'll ruin us again."

His father took a swallow of wine as though trying to control himself. "You talk like I had thirty thousand head instead of a few hundred old ewes."

"Yes, and those few hundred ewes can ruin us just as quickly now," his mother said. "These are poor times, you know."

His father looked down at the table so that no one could see his eyes. "We had *our* Depression a long time ago," he said. "What's happening now don't scare me a bit."

Instead of pacifying his mother as they were intended to do, the dismissing words only inflamed her more. "It can happen again! We've got little enough money to keep this house and feed these kids."

Now his father was getting angry, too. "You'll talk different when we sell the lambs and I bring home a big check!" He caught himself then, abruptly. Putting down his napkin, he got to his feet. Without looking at their mother, he muttered, "You know, it's a sin to fight at table."

And he left, stopping only long enough to pick his Stetson off the peg beside the kitchen door. They heard his long footsteps going down the length of the alley to the back yard, the grinding start of the motor, and the fading roar as the truck drove away.

It was a silent meal. No one dared look at their mother. She pieced grimly at her dinner, then gave it up and took her plate into the kitchen. Pete choked down his food. A great weight of guilt was bearing down on him. If he had not made the foolish request of going to see the sheep, the fight would never have happened.

His brother Leon divined his torment. "It was bound to come," he said in a voice their mother could not hear. "Don't worry. He'll get over it in a few days."

But Leon was wrong about that. Their father's pride had been hurt. It would be two long months before they saw him again.

3

His mother's admonition had been repeated so many times that it had become automatic. "Now, remember," she called after Suzette. "You have to stop and rest every few steps. Don't let Pete talk you out of it. He's got no sense."

Suzette nodded, playing wooden Indian with her face. Pete remarked to himself that she had gotten pretty good at covering up for him. For weeks, she had been his guardian in evening walks, after the heat of the day had passed. Pete guessed that his mother would have a heart attack herself if she knew how much walking he had done around the neighborhood in the concealment of dusk. Suzette had been pretty good about it, getting frightened and bossy only once when he had tried running.

This was to be his first sojourn to Main Street. Their supposed destination was the library, so Pete could check out his own books. Since they had moved into the house, his brothers and sisters had taken turns in going to the library and checking out books to satisfy his voracious appetite. As a result, Pete's reading had been varied according to the likes of all of them. Leon had brought him grown-up books which he detested, his brothers Gene and Mike had brought him Tarzan and Jack London and James Oliver Curwood which he loved, and Suzette had brought him sissy books and fairy tales, which the other kids in school seemed to know about but their family didn't. Pete was just as content that they didn't.

Until they had run the gauntlet of the neighborhood, Pete did not raise his eyes from the sidewalk. Once in a while, they passed people who said hello to them. Suzette said hello back politely, but Pete did not say a word. The cloying sympathy in their greetings only made him hate them the more. They had another think coming if they thought they were going to get around him that way.

"You sure have bad manners," Suzette said primly. "Can't you even say hello when people speak to you?"

"Hell with 'em," Pete muttered.

Suzette gasped. "Now you're going to have to go to Confession."

"I'll say an Act of Contrition," Pete said. "Swearing ain't a mortal sin."

"Ain't ain't in the dictionary so you ain't supposed to say it," she intoned.

"Papa says it," said Pete. "So do a lot of people I know." *Or used to know,* he thought to himself.

Suzette adroitly ducked the mention of their father. "Well, I'm sure glad we don't have to talk to *them* anymore."

"Boy, are you getting stuck up," Pete said hotly. "Just like the rest of 'em."

"Who?" demanded Suzette.

Pete had managed to keep his resentment against the neighbors to himself. Sensing he was on dangerous ground, he said curtly, "Forget it."

They had passed out of the range of fancy homes and onto Main Street. Everything came back to Pete as if it were new. The cannon in front of the Heroes Memorial Building was still pointed at the capitol, the Pony Express fountain was still spouting water, and the squaws had moved over to the shady side of the street. In the near distance, the dome of the capitol and the miniature dome in back that marked the library reared above their thick green enclosure of elms. Pete sighed. It had been such a long time since he had sprawled out on the luxuriant grass in the shade of those elms. He sidled a glance at Suzette, wondering if she had guessed his secret. By the stuck-up thrust of her chin, he knew she had not. Discreetly, as they crossed Main Street, he glanced searchingly to right and left.

At first, he could not believe the luck of it. But there, incredibly, was the unmistakable figure in a battered derby hat and worn striped overalls. Buckshot was sitting alone on one of the green wooden benches under the elms. He was slumped forward with his elbows on his knees, staring at the ground. For an instant, Pete had an impression that Buckshot looked forlorn, but he put the thought aside quickly. It was impossible that Buckshot could ever be sad.

He and Suzette passed through the iron grillwork entrance to the capitol grounds. Feigning weariness, Pete said in a voice that was suspicious even to his own ears, "Getting a little short of breath. I better rest for a while."

Suzette was all concern. "Are you all right, Pete? Why didn't you tell me?"

"Well, it just came on all of a sudden," Pete said in a whisper. "I'll be all right in a minute." He swallowed and then ventured it. "I think I'll go over to the bench and sit down."

Lifting her eyes to follow the direction of his gaze, Suzette drew in her breath sharply. "You sneak!" she hissed. "You're not fooling me. You just want to go see *him*."

"Go see who?" Pete said innocently.

"You know who I mean!" cried Suzette. "That dirty old bum of a Buckshot."

"Oh, is that Buckshot?" said Pete, pretending to peer more closely at the figure on the bench. "Well, whattya know."

"You're not fooling me!" Suzette said, her voice rising.

Realizing that something drastic had to be done, Pete staggered as though he were in danger of falling. He recovered himself and said weakly, "I better rest. I'm feeling poorly."

Suzette was a little uncertain now. "I don't believe you."

Pete gently shook off her supporting hand. "I'll be all right in a minute. Why don't you go get me a book while I take a little rest?"

Suzette's last doubt vanished. "I know what you're up to. You sneak!"

But she did not follow after Pete as he made his wobbling way towards the bench. She stared at him for one outraged moment, and then turned on her heel and stalked up the sidewalk. When she had turned the curving corner in the direction of the library, Pete straightened himself and went to the bench and sat down beside Buckshot. The familiar unwashed smell cut through with whiskey was like a homecoming. "Hi, Buck," he said easily.

Buckshot turned his head as if he had just noticed he had company. "Hi, kid," he said without enthusiasm.

"Long time no see," said Pete.

Buckshot thought about that for a moment. "Yeah, I guess it's been a while at that." He lifted his head and inspected Pete. "Oh, I remember," he said. "You were the one who was sick."

"Yeah," Pete said bravely. "But I'm getting better."

"That's good," said Buckshot lamely. "It's no fun to be sick." He lapsed into a brooding silence as if he had forgotten Pete's presence.

A feeling of being let down was beginning to creep over Pete. He rallied against it. "How's Wash these days?"

"Not good," said Buckshot. "He's got the clap."

Pete's spirits rose at hearing the old language. "Oh, well. Wash always had the clap."

"But not like this time," said Buckshot bitterly. "It caught up with him real good. He's gonna die."

Pete was struck silent by the finality in Buckshot's voice. He contemplated Wash's death for what he thought was a proper interval. "How're things with you, Buck?" he said gently.

"Not so good. They're sending me to the poorfarm tomorrow."

The bottom began to fall out of Pete again, and again he fought against it. "Why?" he said angrily.

"Because I'm a burden on the town."

"What about your brother?" said Pete desperately. "Can't he give you some money?"

"He don't want to have nothing to do with me. He's written me off, as they say."

Pete's mind whirled, trying to figure a way out for Buckshot in his dilemma. There was none, and he surrendered to it. "I'm sorry, Buck," he said. "I understand."

Buckshot got up suddenly then, his whiskey-veined eyes gone ugly. "No, you don't understand, kid!" he said. "You don't know nothing about being an old drunk. You and your family and that fancy house my money went to buy."

Pete continued to sit while the waves of numbness washed over him. He wanted to shout after Buckshot that he had never paid for drink or food in the little hotel in his life, and everyone knew it.

But all he could manage was to say chokingly after the retreating figure, "You old bum! You dirty old bum!"

In one instant, Buckshot had wrecked all of Pete's waking dreams of Main Street. Pete wanted desperately to go home, and home was no longer the little hotel, and never would be again.

4

One thing was for certain. It was a caravan the likes of which the neighbors had never seen. Discreetly parted curtains and the sudden raising of window shades showed that.

Pete was mounted behind his father on the big horse that was called Roan. Behind them followed the pack horse, Buck, loaded down with packbags filled with provisions, and over them, two bulky bedrolls tied down with an elaborate crisscrossing of rope. Bringing up the rear was a copper-colored horse called Rowdy, bearing his big brother Leon in the envied saddle, and his younger brother Gene holding on behind. Rowdy at least looked like the horses Pete had seen in the movies at the showhouse. He was fine muscled with long, slender legs. In comparison to him, Roan and Buck seemed as big and unwieldy as elephants. The rump on which Pete was straddled was so wide that he thought he would be split in two before the day was over.

When the caravan left the back yard, Pete deliberately disdained looking back to wave at his mother and sisters and outraged kid brother, Mike, who had been adjudged too young to make the trip. Pete did not look back in case his mother might have a last minute change of mind. It had been touch and go the evening before, when his father had come home in the most unexpected of fashions, riding one horse and leading two others. There had been a tense moment when his mother and father had met, then she in her unexpected way had relented and said simply, "Hello, stranger." And that was the end of that. Then Pete's father had announced that he was going to take the boys to the mountains, because it would be their last chance before school. Pete had closed his eyes and prayed, and just as if his father had divined his thoughts, he added quickly, before it could become an argument, "I want to take *him* especially. It will do him good, and I will keep an eye on him."

Then had followed a furious time of activity, in which great pieces of soiled canvas were spread on the elegant living room carpet and their father showed them how to make up a bedroll with blankets tucked in at the sides and feet, and canvas pulled over that and tucked in, too, and the whole affair fastened with cinches and ropes. When he had cautioned them to take warm jackets they had been skeptical, but he had said, "You'll be thankful for them when the sun goes down up there, I'm telling you."

After dinner, Pete had sneaked out unnoticed to pet the horses in the great barn. But in the cavernous darkness, all he had succeeded in doing was to startle Rowdy so that he snorted fearfully and lashed out with his hind legs. Pete had beat an inglorious retreat.

There was something a little inglorious, too, in finally being able to wear the boots that Joe Wabuska had given him, and then not even getting to ride in a saddle. Pete had argued about that, but his father said firmly, "Leon is bigger and stronger than you, so he will have to ride Rowdy."

Leon was having his troubles with Rowdy now, and Pete took satisfaction in it. Rowdy was tossing his head and twisting, and both Leon and Gene were hanging on for dear life. "Don't jerk on those reins," his father admonished them. "Let him have his head. He knows more than you do about where to go."

By the time they had crossed the fields that lay west of town, Pete was beginning to be sure of his balance, so that he could let go of his father's waist and hold on to the tie strings in back of the saddle, pretending they were reins. But when they found the narrow dirt road that climbed into the mountains, and Pete had started to slide off the back of the horse, he abandoned his pride and held on grimly to his father's waist. As the road grew steeper, he discovered quickly why it was that his father could actually prefer such a big and unpretty horse as Roan. Pete felt the powerful haunches working beneath him without ever showing tiredness, while the slender-legged Rowdy seemed to need a rest every few minutes.

Their father stopped the caravan on a bend in the road. With one iron arm, he swung Pete to the ground and then stepped off the stirrup with an ease that struck Pete with wonder. It was as if a part of the horse had become disassociated, so old and familiar a motion it was.

Pete had been too occupied to look back even once in their ascent to the bend in the road. So it was that when his father lifted him down and he turned to look back down, the breath left his body. Over the tops of the pines, the town that was his world was diminished to nothing in the immensity of land that surrounded it. The town lay buried under a green umbrella of cottonwoods and poplars and elms, and the capitol dome that had seemed so lofty from below was only a white protuberance looming out of the foliage. Except for a few outlying fields, the greenery ended with the sentinel poplars on the outskirts of town. Beyond that was nothing but gray sagebrush desert and range upon range of desert hills that became hazy with distance and finally blended together and disappeared into one horizon.

"Ain't it a sight to see?" his father said, and then he lapsed into silence, looking off with his eyes squinting against the sun, his Stetson tipped back so that the widow's peak of black hair was perfectly defined, his long bronzed face at peace. Watching him, Pete wondered at the change that had been worked in him. Gone were the taut, nervous lines and the tormented angry eyes by which he had always known his father at the little hotel. *There must be something here that has changed him,* he thought. But he could not figure out what it could be. So far, all the sensation Pete had felt was one of growing apprehension.

They left the road without warning, at what their father said was the low summit, and plunged into a dark and fathomless forest. At first, there seemed to be a semblance of a trail, and then that, too, was left behind. Now Pete really began to be afraid. As they made their twisting way through the tall pines and along the bases of giant rock formations, a menace seemed to lurk behind every trunk. And upon every great pile of rock, Pete was certain there was a mountain lion waiting to leap down upon them. But the menaces on the hidden sides of trees never materialized, and no lion pounced down to rake them with his fearsome talons. And obviously, his father knew his way with an old familiarity. He threaded his way through the forest without even a pause. He knew where he was going as certainly as if he were crossing Main Street in town.

In a little clearing where water gushed from between two rocks and the tiny stream bed was lined on both sides with lush grass and wild-flowers, his father reined up and announced they would have lunch. When Pete got off this time, he could hardly walk, and he was certain the splitting apart that had been promised was beginning to happen. When he saw that his brothers were no better off, he smiled with secret malice. And then Leon made the mistake of dropping the reins so that he could flop down upon the grass. As if by a signal, Rowdy began backing away. Pete felt his father's fingers close upon his arm and Roan's reins thrust into his hand. "Hold him," he said in a voice that was too quiet, and then he spoke to Leon, "Stay right where you are. Don't jump up."

With one hand raised and making soft sounds with his mouth, his father stepped unhurriedly towards Rowdy. The copper-colored horse looked at him, started to turn away, and then turned his head back again. His father's hand slid up slowly and his fingers curled around the strap that ran down the side of Rowdy's head. There was a barely audible sigh from Pete's father as he caught up the dangling reins. He led Rowdy to a tree, and with the thick lead rope that was looped around the horse's neck, tied him to a branch. As he took Roan's reins from Pete's hands, he said to all of them, but no one in particular, "Don't never let this sorrel free for a minute. He will head down to the valley without no invitation. And then we will be in one hell of a fix."

When the horses were securely tied, but with enough slack in the ropes to allow them to munch on the long grass, the boys sprawled out beside the creek. Their father spread a small square of canvas on the ground, and from a cloth sack that was hanging from his saddle horn, took out cheese and bread and a flask of wine wrapped in damp burlap. He laid them down in the middle of the canvas alongside his pocketknife.

"Cut your own bread and cheese," he said. "You might as well learn to feed yourself."

Leon took up the knife carefully and hefted the round chunk of bread. He was unsure how to start, but knowing him, Pete was sure he was not going to ask. Leon set the bread down on the canvas and began sawing with the knife.

"Not that way," his father said. "You are going to ruin my tablecloth." He made Leon hand him the knife, handle first with the blade down, took the bread in his hands and cut it with a quick, circular motion. And then he cut the cheese in the same way.

When they all had their portions of bread and cheese and rough wine, they squatted down beside the square of canvas and ate. The wind soughed through the pines above them, cut through in a million places by the long green needles, so that the sound was like rushing water. A big bird with a blue body and gray wings and a lordly tuft on his head like a plumed knight scolded them raucously from the safety of a high branch. A squirrel chattered across the clearing, running with his long tail stretched out behind him. A humming bird hovered stationary in the air near a growth of green willow, his invisible wings making a sound like a giant bee. A grasshopper hidden somewhere ticked away like a watch going too fast. All the sounds seemed to go together like music. Pete lay back in the deep grass and wondered if he were beginning to understand.

5

In the afternoon, when Pete had begun to tire, his father had lifted him onto the packhorse and made him lie down on top of the bedrolls. At first he had felt ridiculous, spreadeagled on his back with his hands and feet hooked through the ropes that held the pack together. Then, lulled by the plodding motion under him and the passing succession of treetops closing over him, he had actually gone to sleep. He came awake when his father stopped the horses at a shallow pass high in the Sierra.

"Now, this one is going to be the toughest climb of all," his father said, waving an arm at a stony rim that reared like the sharp backbone of an animal into the sky. "If Rowdy takes a notion to fall," he admonished Leon and Gene in a voice rough with seriousness, "then get the hell off that hoss. Don't think about nothing. Just jump out, but on the uphill side so he don't crush you. If you can, Leon, keep hold of the reins."

After the horses had stopped heaving for breath, they mounted again. As closely as he was holding onto his father's waist, Pete was jerked backwards as Roan began the climb with a jolting lunge. His father's hand whipped around and caught him just in time, clamping him to his back. When Pete was secure again, he looked down and quickly looked away. The ground beside them dropped away into nothing. He caught one glimpse of a dislodged boulder bounding down the sheer side of the mountain, and that was enough to reveal to him what would happen if Roan should fall. Behind him, he heard the hard, clinking scramble of hooves and prayed for his brothers' lives.

And then suddenly they were on solid ground and Pete could look about him. They seemed to be on top of the world. One side fell away to descending forests and the distant valley floor they had left that morning, and the other side to a small blue lake caught in the cup of two mountain ranges. On the exposed rim, the wind tore at their hair and flapped their shirts and blew away the sound of a word as soon as it was uttered. The boulder-strewn ground around them looked as if a war had been fought there, with jagged tree trunks blasted and black from lightning bolts, and dwarfed trees bent and misshapen by the winds. They had conquered the mountain, and Pete finally knew the exultancy he had groped for in his imagination, and never reached, in the stories of adventure that had filled his life.

Dusk had fallen when they traversed the rim and began the gradual descent into a green meadow splashed by lingering patches of snow and sheltered by giant pines. Beneath one of the trees deep in the meadow, they made out the white cone of a tent and the shadow figure of Uncle Joanes moving around a blinking fire. The smell of woodsmoke carried to them on the evening breeze, and with it the wild barking of dogs. They had reached their destination.

6

The fragrance of fresh-cut fir boughs suffused Pete. When they reached camp, their father went out immediately with the camp axe and chopped off a seeming mountain of small branches. Pete and his brothers helped their father carry the branches back to camp.

Swiftly, as if from long practice, their father made mattresses for them, laying one bough upon the other with the sharp chopped ends out, so that they would not stick into the sleeper during the night. Then he threw the bulky bedrolls on top with the admonition that when one made camp, he should get his bed ready before anything else. That way, he could crawl into bed as soon as dinner was done. Their father was right as usual. Filled with fresh air and his feet dragging with weariness, Pete drowsed through dinner and fell into his bed.

Daybreak came like chilling death. The world outside was gray and hopeless and utterly without sound. Through the crack in the canvas that he had pulled over his head in the night, Pete sleepily watched his father making the morning fire. In the gray light, his unshaven face was drained of blood and his black mane of hair was wild and uncombed. In back of him, the sky to the west still held a receding blackness.

Kneeling on the ground, his father took a scrap of paper from his pocket and wrapped it in dry pine needles and placed the bundle in the fire pit. Twigs came next in a tiny pyramid. He touched a wooden match to the paper, and when the fire had taken, he crisscrossed sticks of wood on top. While the flames roared up, he filled the blackened coffeepot with water and then dug into a white sack for handfuls of coffee which he dropped into the water. By that time the flames had died down enough for him to put on the curved fire iron, balancing it on the flat rocks on either side of the fire pit. The coffeepot came next and the flames enveloped it like a Viking's bier.

His father sensed that he was being observed and his gray eyes rose up to meet Pete's. "Did you hear the winds fighting in the night?" he said in a low voice so as not to awaken the others.

Pete nodded, remembering. He had roused once to hear the winds raging in the night. They had unsettled him and he had burrowed down into the woolen blankets and pressed his back against his brother's for reassurance.

"They fought a big battle on the rim up there, the west wind and the east wind," his father said. "It looked for a while like the east wind was going to win. But in the end, the west wind was too strong for him."

He fell silent then and knelt without moving, as if waiting for something to happen. The leaves began to flutter and a cool trembling breeze sprang up, coming out of nowhere and going nowhere so that the very air contained it and shook with it. A golden shaft of light drove into the camp like a sword, dispelling as if by magic the gray hopelessness of the daybreak. The air was suddenly flooded with the unleashed scents of growing things. A thousand waiting birds seemed to burst all at the same moment into a shrilling chorus of song. From their bedground in the meadow above them, a lamb welcomed the first warmth with a quavering bleat. The day had begun.

"Come and have your coffee," his father said. "We got work in front of us. With you boys here to help, it's a good chance to count the sheep."

Crawling reluctantly out of the bedroll he had shared with Leon, Pete pulled on his pants and shoes. The battered metal wash basin was set on a stump with a towel hanging nearby. As he had seen Uncle Joanes do, Pete filled the basin sparingly with water from the canteen. The icy shock of it brought him awake in a hurry.

His father filled his tin cup with coffee that had barely come to a boil in the fire-blackened coffeepot. Sweetening it with canned milk and sugar from a small white sack, Pete dipped a huge chunk of sourdough bread into the mixture. He chewed the thick crust carefully. When he was done, he wiped his hands on his pants, thinking, *No napkins. Now, this is the way I want to live.*

Pete supposed they helped some with the counting of the sheep, but the shaggy dogs did most of the work, barking and turning runaways back into the main band with reproving nips at hindquarters and ears of the sheep. They at least knew what they were doing.

7

Like Indians, they came trudging back through the deep forest in single file. The shaggy, tireless dogs ranged out in front, and their Uncle Joanes brought up the rear because he had an obsession about the boys wandering off and getting lost. They were covered with the brown wood dust that the sheep had stirred up when they were being counted. Pete and his brothers had stayed in back and on the flanks of the band, shouting and waving their hands to drive the sheep into a narrow space against a mound of high rocks, where their father had counted them and Uncle Joanes had notched a stick every time a hundred sheep went by. When the counting was done, the sheep lay down in the shade to take their noonday rest, and their Uncle Joanes had said, "And I will take a lunch and rest, too, if I can be sure of some peace and quiet."

Pete could not figure out his Uncle Joanes. He always seemed to look at the dark side of things. And he was cranky, reprimanding the boys at every turn, although he must have realized they could not be expected to know anything about sheep. It surprised Pete that his father did not come to their defense. Pete had said to his father, "Why is he always so mad?" But his father had merely shrugged and said, "He ain't really mad. That's just his nature. He gets so nervous if things don't go his way. I don't want to talk against my own brother, but I will tell you this about him. If there is anything Joanes hates, it is a mean hoss. But if a hoss ain't mean when he gets him, he is sure as hell mean when Joanes gets rid of him."

Guided by their father, they had taken a shortcut through the forest so they would come out right at the camp. As he said later, the reason the dogs did not smell the bear was because the wind was not in their favor.

The first sign that something was wrong was when their father stopped abruptly at the last fringe of trees and said in a voice taut with warning, "Stay back!" At the same instant, the dogs burst into frenzied barking. Their father tried to contain them, but it was too late. Hackles up and fangs bared, the dogs were streaking toward the camp. "Goddam!" their father swore. "They are going to get him mad."

Despite a warning, Pete crowded up behind his father. A huge something with rippling black fur and a long snout was moving around inside the camp. It did not seem to notice the dogs until they were almost upon it, and then it whirled and raised itself upright like a man. Pete felt the short hairs at the back of his neck go stiff with recognition.

The big red dog, Campolo, was the first one to reach the camp. He left the ground in a running leap for the bear's throat. He might as well have run into a stone wall. The bear took the full impact of Campolo's charge without even a backward step. Campolo bounced off the bear's chest and fell sideways to the ground. In one fluid motion, the bear leaned down and swiped at him. The blow caught Campolo on the shoulder and hurled him through the air like a rag doll.

The other dog, Neshka, was slower and wiser. She came to a skidding stop and contented herself with furious snarling just outside the bear's reach. The bear made one step toward her and then, for the first time, seemed to sense the presence of humans. He opened his mouth wide to show his long white fangs, snarled hideously, and sank down on his four legs. He left the camp unhurriedly, but once he was beyond it, he broke into a lumbering run, looking back only once to see if he were being pursued.

As soon as the bear started to run, Pete's father strode rapidly toward the camp, took the carbine down from where it was hanging on the tree, and checked the load. The bear was still very much in sight when Pete and his brothers and Uncle Joanes reached the camp. "Aren't you going to shoot him?" cried Pete.

"No," his father said. "I was just getting ready in case he changed his mind and decided to pay us another visit."

The bear had almost gained the trees at the far end of the meadow. "Why don't you shoot him?" Pete shouted.

His father regarded him with something close to anger, then caught himself and said quietly, "He don't kill our sheep. Why should I kill him?"

Pete bent his head, but only to hide his disappointment in his father. Turning away, he went to where Neshka was already licking Campolo's wounds. The bear reached the concealment of the trees, but Pete did not care enough anymore even to watch him disappear.

8

"Hey, Pete!" his kid brother Gene called from the bank of the tiny stream that flowed below the camp. "Look what I found."

Pete was not interested in what Gene had found. He was stretched out on the bedroll where he had pretended to be asleep when his Uncle Joanes had gone back to watch the sheep and his father had taken off down the canyon to retrieve the horses. Hobbled and all, they had managed to cover a lot of ground when the bear invaded the camp.

Lunch had been a big omelette with green peppers and onions and scraps of bacon and fried potatoes all thrown in together. His father had ignored him coldly, and that had taken away Pete's appetite. He was ashamed for shouting at his father and yet angry with him for cheating them out of seeing a wild bear shot to death.

Pete lay on his back and scowled at the clumps of pine needles quivering against the blue sky. The sound of his brother Leon's regular breathing from where he slept on another bedroll irritated him, and the whimperings of Campolo did not move him to pity. He wished he had not even come to the mountains, but instead, stayed home where he could be assured of some sympathy.

Gene's grinning face suddenly loomed over him, blocking out the pine needles. He was for sure excited about something. Pete deigned to look at him. Gene was holding a rusted can with his hand clamped over the top of it.

"Why didn't you come down to the creek?" said Gene.

"Why should I?" said Pete indifferently.

"All right, then," said Gene. "I won't show you."

Curiosity tugged at Pete. "Whatcha got?" he said reluctantly.

In answer, Gene slid the palm of his hand partly off the top of the can. At first, nothing happened. Then a tiny creature with long hind legs leaped through the aperture. Pete ducked and threw up his hands.

"Chicken," said Gene mockingly. "It's only a frog."

Pete sat up on the bedroll. Resting in a fold of canvas was the tiniest frog he had ever seen. He eased his hand forward slowly and plopped it over the frog, picking it up. When he turned his hand over, the frog did not try to jump. It seemed content to rest comfortably in Pete's palm. Pete bent forward to examine it. It had liquid eyes and brilliant green markings on its back. "Well, I'll be darned," Pete exclaimed. "Where'd you find him?"

"In the creek," said Gene. "I caught six of 'em."

"Lemme see."

"Can't," said Gene. "They'll get away."

"Well, what good are they if you can't see 'em?" said Pete. Glancing around the camp for a receptacle big enough to hold the frogs, his eyes lighted on the blackened frying pan resting on the fire iron. It was big and round and had high sides. "Let's put 'em in the frying pan."

"No!" recoiled Gene. "I don't want to kill 'em."

"I didn't mean that," said Pete. "It's the only thing big enough."

Gene surveyed the frying pan. "Okay."

They put the frying pan on the ground and hunkered down on both sides of it. Pete put his frog inside and Gene turned the rusted can over and emptied its contents inside, too. The frogs lay where they had fallen, blinking their eyes and not making any effort to move. Pete prodded one, but all he gave was a little hop.

"They're sure not jumpers," said Pete.

"That's because they're babies," said Gene with an air of authority.

"Mine jumped out of the can," said Pete.

"He's not yours," said Gene. "They're all mine."

Pete stood up. "I guess I could go down and catch one for myself."

"Oh, keep him then," said Gene, and Pete squatted down again. The frogs were making no effort to move and Pete was getting bored.

"I bet I know how to make 'em jump," he said. "Let's put the frying pan on the fire."

"No!" said Gene. "That'll burn their feet."

"We'll put some water inside so they don't get too hot," said Pete. "That'll do the trick."

Gene pondered the proposition. "Well, if you're sure they won't burn their feet," he said hesitantly.

Beneath the gray ashes in the firepit there were still a few coals. As he had seen his father do, Pete placed a handful of dry twigs on the coals and blew them into a flame. From the canteen, he poured water into the frying pan. Carefully, so that the frogs would not spill out, he lifted the pan and set it on the fire iron.

"See what I told you," said Pete. "They're sure jumping now."

The words had hardly escaped from his mouth when it happened. Heated by the flames underneath, the water had mixed with the film of grease in the frying pan to form a paste. The paste bubbled up to encase the back feet of the frogs so that they were stuck to the bottom of the pan. The frogs leaped to the full length of their bodies, but their hind legs held them fast. One by one, the leaping bodies separated themselves from their legs, leaving white flesh and dangling tendons and muscles behind.

"Oh, my God!" moaned Pete. Beside him, Gene covered his eyes with his hands and burst into tears. In desperation, Pete grasped the handle of the frying pan. He jerked it away with a yell as the metal seared into his hand. Then, gritting his teeth, he reached forward again and pulled the frying pan off the fire iron and onto the dirt.

Drawn by the stench and the yell, Leon found them huddled over the frying pan and its grizzly contents. "Jesus!" he began, but whatever else he was going to say was bitten back by Gene's convulsive sobs and the sight of Pete's blistered hand.

Without another word, Leon took up a piece of sacking and wrapped it around the handle of the frying pan. On his way out of camp, he picked up a shovel. Beyond the fringe of trees, they could hear the concealing of their crime.

In the days that followed, Pete never knew for sure if his father guessed at what had happened between them and the frogs. By the time he came back up the canyon leading the horses, Pete had scrubbed out the frying pan with soap and water and put it back exactly where he had found it on the fire iron. Even so, it seemed to Pete that the smell of burning frogs hung over everything.

When his father had finished rehobbling the horses and turning them loose in the meadow, he came walking back to the camp. Pete had realized long ago that he was no good at dissimulation, even when he was innocent of something that his brothers were guilty of. He sensed now that his posture, and Gene's, were a dead giveaway. He and Gene were sitting huddled together like conspirators on a bedroll, and Leon was lying on another bedroll, his back turned on them in cold disapproval.

Their father took one look at Pete and said in instant concern, "You're white as a sheet. Is your heart giving you trouble?"

Pete shook his head, thinking to himself, *I only wish it was.*

Then their father's gray eyes swerved toward Gene. The dust on Gene's face was streaked with tears. Their father's brow furrowed and he started to say something. Then he clamped his mouth shut. Pete could have sworn that his nostrils quivered, because his father's gaze went to the frying pan. Pete looked at it, too, wondering what his father's eyes were finding wrong. Pete's heart gave a leap. The bottom of the frying pan, which was always kept moist and shining with grease, was dry as a bone.

Their father was lost in thought for a long moment and then he went to tend to Campolo's wounds, daubing them with strong-smelling sheep dip. If he suspected something, he never mentioned it during the rest of their stay at the mountain sheepcamp. If they had done something bad, there was nothing their father could do that would add to their punishment.

9

For one last time they had gone to the biggest of the summer snow banks in the upper meadow. Knowing what was in store for him, Leon had joined Pete and Gene with reluctance. After sliding down on the track they had worn smooth with the seats of their pants, there would be the inevitable snowball fight. Since Leon was the biggest, he would have to stand off the combined assault from Pete and Gene.

Now, he stood his ground resolutely with a dripping snowball in either hand and a reserve supply stacked up in front of him. Below, Pete and Gene were circling warily so as to crossfire him from opposite sides. Gene was the best thrower, but Pete was the most reckless when he had his blood up. Always before, Leon had stood sideways to Gene to offer the least target. But this time he decided to change his tactic of defense and stood ready to return Pete's fire. It would be Pete who would start the attack, and he did so now, his snowball going predictably wild. Leon let the throw pass over his head, then whirled and pumped his first snowball at Gene. Off guard, Gene caught the missile of coarse-grained snow in the pit of his stomach. He sank down to his knees, dropping all of his ammunition so he could clutch his stomach. Seeing his ally go down, Pete cast aside all caution and charged. Leon braced himself to meet the assault. Then, abruptly, he straightened and raised his hand. "Hold it!" he cried.

Pete stopped in his tracks and turned to see what Leon was staring at. It was their father emerging from the forest with a lamb draped over his shoulders. The sight was surprising because the sheep, and especially the lambs, were so wary that he could not even get close to them. Pete made no connection at all between the live lamb and the marbled carcass shrouded in a long flour sack and hanging from a tree limb at the camp. The carcass was simply something that was constantly being whittled at to provide meat for their evening meals. There wasn't much left of it now.

"I guess he must be hurt or something," said Leon.

"I bet a coyote got him," said Pete. "Let's go see."

The snowball fight was forgotten, and so was Gene. Struggling for breath, he saw himself being deserted on the snowbank. Complaining at the lack of compassion in his brothers, he forced himself to his feet and trailed after them, still bent over with the pain in his stomach.

Their father had deposited the lamb on the ground under the big tree. His forelegs were tied together; and so were the hind ones. Pete bent over to inspect him at close quarters. His head was covered with tightly curled white wool, but his ears and nose were black. He was so fat that his eyes were bright little slits in his face. Pete stretched his hand forward and touched the lamb's nose. It was soft and moist to his fingertips. When Pete explored further, rubbing his hand on the curling wool between his ears, the lamb jerked away and made a bleating sound that was almost like a mew, and then submitted to the rubbing. Pete was enthralled. It was the first lamb he had ever touched. A fantastic thought crossed his mind. The reason his father had caught the lamb was to take him home as a pet for the family.

"He doesn't look hurt," said Leon, who had squatted down beside him. "And he doesn't look sick, either." He called to their father, "What's the matter with him, Papa?"

Their father had been busying himself throwing a loop of rope over a low-hanging limb. He glanced over his shoulder at the boys and said with a peculiar note in his voice, "I wish you would stay away from him." As soon as he had said the words, Campolo raised his head from the big wool sack where he was lying and barked sharply. Later, Pete was to remember that Campolo's bark held the same peculiar note as his father's voice. It was as if something had passed between them that no one else could understand.

Their father came now to stand over them. "I think you better go gather some firewood."

"Aw, Papa! Why?" Pete cried out. "We want to play with our lamb."

"He *is* our lamb, isn't he?" said Gene.

"I guess so," their father mumbled. There was a distressed expression on his face.

"Then we ought to give him a name," said Pete. "I choose Spotty because he's got a black spot right there." And Pete put his finger on it.

Their father regarded them gravely. Then he seemed to come to a decision. "Well, I guess you better start getting used to it now," he said, taking a deep breath. "Give me some room."

He kneeled down then in the dirt and wedged one knee on a spot between the lamb's shoulder and its neck. When the lamb was pinioned, he reached into his pocket and pulled out his knife. When he opened it, it was to reveal the long blade freshly honed to a gleam.

I know what, thought Pete. *He is going to take a thorn out of our lamb's foot.*

"Poor thing," his father said, and plunged the long blade into the lamb's throat.

Pete did not move. He could not move if he had wanted to. Seeing and not really seeing, he watched the fresh red blood gush out over his father's hand and onto the ground. He saw the lamb's legs kicking with a terrible strength against the thongs that bound him. And he saw the brightness go out of the lamb's eyes and the dull glaze of death come into them.

Pete raised his head. Another set of eyes met his. They were his father's and they said, *Now, don't you see why I don't want to kill when I don't have to.*

A · U · T · U · M · N

10

Before I let you out for recess," Miss Elliott said in her simpering voice, "I must caution you to be careful with Pete. He has a weak heart, you know. The doctor has advised me that he is not allowed to play at any rough games. I take that to mean football and baseball. So, you boys especially will have to be careful not to coax Pete to join in your games. I am counting on the girls to make sure that Pete . . ."

As the incredible words made worse by sugar sweetness droned on and on, describing the ravages of his sickness and the terrible consequences of it, Pete sank lower and lower in his seat. His ears were burning as if they were on fire, and he could not look up because he knew that every eye in the room was turned in his direction. There had even been a mean, low laugh from someone when Miss Elliott asked the girls to watch over him. Pete had a good idea from whom it had come.

He trailed out of the room with his head hanging. Down the long, dim hallway, nobody spoke a word to him. He stepped out onto the big stone steps into the golden autumn sun, and Tony was waiting for him. When school had started that morning, Tony had raised his chin in a gesture that said hello and nothing more. In the nine months since Pete had gotten sick, Tony had not come to see him once. Pete could understand that. Tony just didn't go into people's houses. It was not his way. Now that they were on neutral ground, Tony would talk to him. "She's full of shit," were the first words he spoke. "Do you want me to sit with you?"

Pete shook his head, too miserable to raise his eyes. He watched Tony's worn shoes turn and go down the steps. They were replaced by two pairs of saddle shoes, still new and unscuffed. "I bet Tony was trying to get you to play football," said a piping voice. "We're going to tell Miss Elliott on him."

There was a clucking chorus of approval. Pete's head flew up. It was as he had guessed. He was surrounded by girls. "You'll be telling a lie!" he blazed.

The girls were taken aback by his anger, but only for a moment.

"We'll sit with you, Pete," said Beverly Schultz, her round face and blue eyes framed by ringlets.

"Did it hurt much, Pete?" another voice said. "I bet it hurt terribly, you poor boy."

"My mother says you'll never be able to run again," said another voice.

"That's a lie!" Pete shouted.

The ring of girls fell silent again. Then a voice he did not recognize from before spoke up. It was not a clinging voice filled with pity. "You don't look sick to me," it said. "How come you're so sunburned if you're sick?"

Pete's searching gaze found the source of the voice. It was the new girl who had been introduced to the class that morning. Her name was Helen something-or-other, and she looked like a tomboy. She was not tall, but thin, with wide shoulders and sprouting breasts that she did not bother to conceal with ruffled blouses. She had short hair that was bleached with the sun, her eyes were flecked with green, and she had some sort of wire contraption on her teeth. She regarded him steadily, unmoved by his fury.

"I'm not sick," he heard himself saying. "If I was sick, how could I go to the mountains on a horse and almost get killed falling off a cliff and sleep outside in the snow and chase wild sheep and almost get eaten by a bear and . . ." He would have gone on, but a familiar and hated face had insinuated itself among the girls.

"D'you wear hip boots when you chase sheep?" said Jimmy Secombe in the tormenting voice he remembered so well. As if in explanation, he nudged the girl next to him. "You know what they say about sheep-herders."

It was a moment before Pete understood what Jimmy Secombe had said. Then the meaning broke over him with a white light. He remembered nothing after that until he felt the principal's big hands shaking him, but uncertainly as if afraid to go too far.

The faces of girls had been transformed as if by a miracle into the grinning faces of impressed boys. Then Pete tasted blood in his mouth and felt the burning from where his knuckles had been scraped bare. Jimmy Secombe was sitting in the dirt in front of him. His face was bloody and his eyes were already swelling shut, but they were still open enough to reveal the fear that filled them.

Afterwards, Miss Elliott glanced at him more than usual as she was teaching. She seemed disappointed, as though the fight had robbed her of something. Pete returned her gaze stoically. There was one thing he was sure of. There would be no more mention of weak hearts. He was suffused with warmth, remembering what Tony had said to him in the washroom. "Jesus H. Christ," he had said. "I thought you were gonna kill him." And then there was the new girl, who had waited purposely outside the classroom to say to him teasingly, "You wanna wrestle?" And then, in a different tone, "Hey, we're gonna play kick-the-can tonight after supper. In case you didn't know, we're neighbors."

Pete sighed and regarded the mercurochrome that had been daubed on his knuckles. Altogether, his first day back at school had turned out just fine.

11

Pete did not even have to sneak out of the house. Ever since he had come back from the mountains, it was as if his mother had pronounced him well. There had not been one recurrence of the visits in the middle of the night, when his mother would crack the bedroom door and wait until she heard his breathing before she went back to bed. Gone also was the worry that narrowed her eyes whenever she looked at him. Now he was on the same level as the others, with the same privileges and the same punishments. At first, he had not been quite certain whether he liked his new station. But there were times of compensation, too, and tonight was one of them.

The evening was warm with lingering Indian summer and the air rich with the heavy scents of overripe flowers. Something else was added, though, or at least it had been when he left the house and felt the velvet night close around him. It was a deep stirring of anticipation, as though a secret waited for him in the night. Casting around for what it could be, he decided that it had to do with the new girl. But when they gathered in the glow of the overhanging street lamp, she ignored him as if he did not exist. That dashed him down for a moment, and then he got angry and ignored her, too.

The can clattered away on the hard-packed street, and all the shadowy figures poised for flight scattered with muffled cries into the night. Pete fled to the protection of one of the giant cottonwoods that lined the street. He ducked behind it, taking care to keep the trunk of the tree between him and the revealing light from the street lamp. The sound of approaching footsteps told him he had not run far enough. Abandoning caution, he made for the corner of a big white house. When he paused, breathing hard, he heard the footsteps still in pursuit. He told himself it did not make sense. Rick, the kid who was *It*, should not be venturing that far from home base. Still, Pete was not taking any chances. He turned and ran blindly across the rolling lawn in back. The silent spray of an unseen sprinkler flew up around him and he emerged gasping on the other side. Behind him, he heard a yelp of surprise. Whoever was pursuing him had made the same mistake, and the high pitched cry told him it was not who he thought it was.

Pete waited until the slight, panting figure, sopping wet with water, came up to him. "What're you following me for?" he hissed. "He'll catch us both that way."

"No, he won't," whispered Helen. "I know a perfect place to hide."

A warm, soft hand slipped into his and led him away. They did not go far. At the back of the lot, an unpainted shed loomed in front of them. Helen seemed to know exactly where she was. Pete heard the big iron hook on the door scrape against its slot and the shed door creak open. He let himself be led inside by the urging handclasp.

The shed was musty with the smell of old wood and neglected leather and rotting straw. As his eyes grew accustomed to the deeper darkness, Pete made out the shape of a horse buggy fallen into disrepair. There were pitchforks and shovels standing in the corner, and harness and nosebags hanging from the wall. By the dim light from a tiny window laced with cobwebs, Pete saw the outline of a ladder that led to a loft. When Helen had gotten back her breath, it was to the ladder that she led him.

"We're safe enough here," Pete protested.

"No," whispered Helen. "He'll catch us for sure."

She clambered up the ladder as though she were sure of every rung. Pete followed her dumbly. He had seen the flash of brown legs ending in white where her panties should have been, and realized that as far as Helen was concerned, the game was forgotten. When he gained the loft, it was to see her sitting on the straw with her skirt spread demurely over her knees.

"We'll be safe here," she said, and then added in a voice gone husky, "Come sit down."

He walked to her on stiff legs, trying to conceal what was happening to him. When he saw her eyes travel downward to the level of his belt, he knew that he had been unsuccessful. But the strange thing was that she did not seem to be at all embarrassed.

As he sat down beside her on the straw, the heavy feeling that had been creeping upwards from his loins turned his limbs leaden. When he turned to look at her, he saw expectation in her eyes. He knew an instant of panic. He was helpless to do anything because he did not know what he was supposed to do. Her expression turned to one of exasperation. "I bet you've never even kissed a girl," she said accusingly.

He heard his own voice come out in a croak. "Sure I have."

"Well then, do it."

Awkwardly, his mouth found hers. It was hard and eager, writhing under his lips like something alive. He felt her hand grasp his and slip it under her blouse and onto her tiny breast. Afraid to hurt her, he let his hand rest where she had placed it. Her mouth parted from his for the fraction of a second it took her to say, "Do something. Don't just hold it."

He did so, squeezing the incredible tenderness of it under his hand. Then everything happened at once. He did not have to do anything. Her hands dropped down and unbuckled his belt and undid the buttons more rapidly than he could have himself. She fell back on the straw, dragging him down on top of her and lifting her hips up only long enough to pull the skirt above her buttocks. She reached down and grasped his prick and guided it into her, and then her naked legs locked around him. As the moist warm softness enveloped him, his eyes rolled up in his head. It seemed he had barely entered her when all the life in his body traveled down to his groin, lingered there for one numbing moment and exploded.

When it was over, he lay spent between her thighs. She pulled her legs together and shoved him away. "You could've done it longer," she said bitterly. "I didn't even get started. Boy, the hicks in this town. They don't even know how to fuck."

But he was filled with the most overpowering love he had ever known for anybody or anything in his life, and the words held no import for him.

12

All the long week after the kick-the-can game, the premonition that Sunday was going to be a bad day had been growing on Pete. His nights had alternately been filled with the ecstatic torment of how it had been in the hayloft with Helen and the heavy knowledge that he had committed a mortal sin.

The days in school had not been much better. He feared that his sin showed so clearly in his face that he might as well have been wearing a sign announcing it to all. When nobody said anything, either in words or by a knowing smirk, he convinced himself that his classmates were lying in wait to unmask him publicly at an opportune moment. Every time someone raised a hand to answer a question in class, Pete's body constricted, certain that their first words would be, "Miss Elliott, I think everybody in this class should know that Pete fucked Helen." And wheel around to fix him with a quivering finger of accusation.

As for Helen, her attitude confounded him absolutely. The morning after it had happened he avoided her as if she had leprosy, not even daring to meet her eyes. But from the vantage point of his seat in the classroom he had watched her covertly over the top of his book. Her appearance and demeanor should have changed radically. He was not certain how or where the change should reveal itself, but one did not do what they had done without changing. Instead, she was as cool and composed as if nothing out of the ordinary had taken place. She did not walk any differently or talk any differently, and never once had she shown the least inclination of doing what he dreaded she would do— throw her arms around him and announce to everyone, "Pete and I are just the same as married people."

When finally they did confront each other, Helen regarded him with nothing showing in her eyes, just as if he were any old classmate. That more than anything else struck his pride, and the secret love he bore her turned to anger and then to downright hate.

With the burden of guilt and fear that he had had to carry all week, the fact that Confession night was approaching completely escaped him. The awful realization came at dinner on Saturday night, when his mother intoned her weekly instruction, "Now, you boys bring your sisters home right after Confession."

Because there was no escape from it, Pete had trudged dutifully to the church. And dutifully he had kneeled down under the guise of doing his Examination of Conscience. There was really no need for that. He knew what he had to confess. He caught himself thinking nostalgically about the sins he had thought were so grievous before. Taking the name of the Lord in vain and losing his temper and having a wet dream paled now into insignificance.

When his turn came, Pete almost rose to his feet to take the fatal plunge into the black-shrouded confessional. Then he had knelt again quickly. When this happened a second time, he could feel the eyes of his brothers and sisters upon him. He ignored the thrusting elbow of Leon and the irritated whisper, "Hurry up. We're all done."

"Well, go outside then," Pete managed to mutter through his praying hands. "I'll be there in a minute."

But he had deceived himself that he could muster the courage when his brothers and sisters were outside the church. He knelt transfixed until there were only three people remaining in the church. Leon came in again and kneeled down beside him. "Why're you taking so long?"

"I'm not through with my Examination of Conscience," Pete whispered hopelessly.

Leon was silent as if he were thinking. Then he got up and whispered knowingly, "I bet you're not."

It was then Pete decided he was not going to Confession this night. He would wait until the Confession before Mass the next morning. Either that or run away or kill himself. He waited a reasonable interval, then he crossed himself and left the church.

Believing that Pete had gone to Confession, his brothers and sisters asked him no questions on the walk home. All except Leon, who fell back with Pete and said out of hearing of the others, "Did you go to Confession?"

"None of your beeswax," said Pete.

But the next morning was no different. In fact, it was worse. Pete had not reckoned with the fact that the church would not be concealingly dim like the night before. Full, revealing daylight poured through the stained glass windows, and he understood why the main Confession was held at night. Darkness went with the dark business of admitting to sins. He paused only long enough to glance at the confessional, and then with face averted to escape the always-following eyes of the life-size statue of Jesus near the altar, he made his way up the long aisle to the sacristy. When he put on the red cassock that was too long, his mind was in such a turmoil that he forgot to take up a tuck in the skirts so that he could walk without tripping. By the time he discovered his omission, it would be too late.

His premonition that it was going to be a bad day was confirmed before Sunday Mass had properly begun. Because Pete was the first altar boy to be dressed, the cantankerous old Irish priest, Father O'Malley, ordered him to light the altar candles. Pete went out to perform the task before the watching eyes of a church full of people. Despite his unsteady hands, he managed to light the first candle. But when he came to the second candle, he did not notice that one fern from the altar flowers was hanging directly over the wick. The wick lighted dutifully and the fern followed suit. Pete could only stand and watch the spreading fire in fascination. A collective sound of alarm from the congregation brought him to his senses. The only thing he could think of to do was grasp the flaming fern in his hands. The motion toppled the vase, putting out the fire, all right, but also dousing Pete with a cascade of water and flowers. While the congregation tittered, Pete went down on his knees to pick up the flowers and put them back in the vase and then put the vase back on the altar. Dimly, he heard a new burst of tittering from the congregation, but he could not figure out the reason for it.

An apoplectic Father O'Malley enlightened him when Pete finally made it back to the sacristy. "What in hell is going on out there?" he hissed. "What in hell is that flower doing in your hair? And how in hell did you get all wet?"

Unable to answer a single question, let alone a multitude of them, Pete simply stared at him. Father O'Malley took a deep breath, reached out to remove the flower from Pete's head, and said in a choking voice, "All right! Let's get this show on the road."

The ritual of the Mass and the comforting flow of Latin took on its familiar pattern, and Pete told himself that perhaps God was through punishing him. Very soon, he realized he was mistaken. When the time came for him to move the huge book of the Mass from the epistle side to the gospel side, he managed the first half of it without mishap, genuflecting at the foot of the altar and going up to get the book and making it back down to the foot of the altar again for another genuflection. Then, disaster struck. When he rose from his knee and began the ascent with the book to the gospel side, he discovered an instant too late that he was walking up the inside of the long cassock. The holy book flew out into space and Pete fell flat at Father O'Malley's feet. There was an exclamation of horror from the congregation that drowned out Father O'Malley's curse. His vestments flapping, he retrieved the book. There was no helping hand for Pete. Disengaging the tangled skirts of the cassock, he crept on hands and knees to the server's position.

Still one more ordeal was left for him. When the time came for Communion, it was protocol for the senior server to receive the wafer first. Pete had desperately tampered with the idea of taking the host even though he had not gone to Confession. But the fact of committing sacrilege and the prospect of eternal damnation was too much to cope with. At the last moment, he looked helplessly up into Father O'Malley's furious eyes and shook his head.

"Why aren't you taking Communion?" Father O'Malley said in a stage whisper that must have carried to the choir.

"I forgot to make Confession," Pete blurted out with inspiration.

Father O'Malley seemed undecided for a moment. Then he whispered harshly, "I'll see you after Mass. You can make Confession then."

When the church was emptied, Pete knelt in a back pew and surrendered himself to his fate. The shuffling of Father O'Malley's feet inside the confessional was growing impatient. Pete took a deep breath and walked like a condemned man to the shrouded curtains, parted them, and knelt down. "Bless me, Father, for I have sinned," he began.

"All right, all right. Make it quick," said an invisible Father O'Malley from the other side of the wire mesh. "I haven't had breakfast."

"I uh . . . I uh . . . did something with a girl, Father."

Father O'Malley heard him with an impatient sniff. "You better lay off that stuff," he said. "Kissing can lead to trouble." He sniffed again and said, "All right, say a good Act of Contrition. Your penance is one rosary."

Pete could not believe his good fortune. Before it was lost to him, he began his Act of Contrition. Too eagerly, he decided later, because Father O'Malley interrupted him with a beginning suspicion in his voice. "Just a minute there. Just exactly what did you do with this girl?"

The world crumbled around Pete's shoulders, but there was no escape now. In the back of his mind, he found himself wishing there were another word for it. But he did not know any other word. "I fucked her."

The confessional rocked as if it had been caught up in an earthquake. When Father O'Malley could speak again, all he could say was, "What? What? What?" It seemed to go on forever.

When it was over, Pete knelt in the empty church, reciting his penance of ten rosaries. His ears were still ringing from Father O'Malley's denunciation. It occurred to Pete that for a priest, Father O'Malley had an uncommon knowledge of cuss words.

He remembered something else Father O'Malley had said that puzzled him. "If anybody in your family thinks I'm going to make a priest out of you, they got another think coming. There'd be nothing left of Holy Mother Church in a week, much less the shambles that would be left in the conduct of Holy Mass. So forget it!"

Pete could not imagine where Father O'Malley had gotten the idea that he should be a priest. He guessed his mother probably had something to do with it. Well, if she had that misconception, she would be cured of it very soon after learning that he had been kicked out of the altar boys. He could not be certain, but he hoped she would put his expulsion down to his performance at Sunday Mass.

Repeating the endless rosaries without paying proper attention to penitence, it occurred to Pete that for such a pleasureful thing, the aftermath of fucking could sure get complicated.

W · I · N · T · E · R

13

The Depression came home to Pete in the form of a penny postcard delivered by an embarrassed mailman on a Saturday morning.

Before that, Depression had been a grown-up word mentioned only rarely by their mother, who seemed to be guarding them from it, and more often in class by Miss Elliott, who would say by way of nothing, with a doleful droop to the corners of her mouth, "The country is in a depression."

At such times, it was as if she had uttered a mystery word that was beyond their comprehension. Thinking that he was singular in his density, Pete would glance at his schoolmates and be reassured. The same puzzlement was registered on the faces of those who had even taken the pains to listen.

Pete guessed that it had to do with one of two things. It was either that nobody had any money in his pocket or, somehow, that people's lives had changed. If it had to do with the first, Pete could not remember when he had any great use for money other than a nickle to buy marbles or the rare times when a whole dime was needed to go to a Saturday afternoon matinee at the showhouse. For that, he and his brothers would make a Saturday morning foray with a gunny sack to collect old Tahoe Beer bottles from neighbors' garages and sell them to the brewery kitty-corner across from the schoolhouse.

If the Depression meant instead that people's lives had changed, Pete wondered about his own. Except for living in a house instead of the little hotel, not much else seemed to have changed. He had been in the house long enough by now that everything had fallen into a routine, and he barely recalled everyday life at the hotel.

In the cold mornings, his mother would wake up first to light the wood stove in the kitchen. Now that winter was approaching, the living room and the bedrooms were closed off in order to keep the heat confined. After they had gone to school, she would light the big wood stove in the dining room so that it would be warm when they came home for lunch and dinner. In the evenings, they would study and play and listen to the radio by the warmth of the big stove, and then brave themselves for the dash to cold bedrooms and icy sheets.

But it was the morning warmth that Pete liked the best, when he would run shivering into the kitchen and soak up the dry wood heat that radiated off the cast-iron plates and stare as if hypnotized at the flickering lines of fiery red that showed through the chinks.

By then, his mother had made the coffee and the mush, and the first one up was sent to the front porch to bring in the milk. Pete would wake up especially so that he could see the bottles. Each morning as the weather grew colder, they took on an unreal aspect. The thick cream at the top would rise out of the bottles so that each one seemed to have grown a neck and a head with a cap perched miraculously on top. One could judge how cold the night had been by the height which the cream had risen. To bring in the milk gave him an added pleasure because he knew it had come from Joe Wabuska's dairy cows.

Pete was vaguely aware that they owed a big milk and butter bill to the Eagle Valley Creamery, but that fact was nothing out of the ordinary. They owed a lot of money to such places as Art Burlingame's shoe store and the grocery store, and less money to people like the doctor and the dentist, because someone had to be really sick before the doctor was called anymore and in such pain from a toothache that oil of cloves would not do the job.

There was some payment money coming in regularly from the people who had bought the little hotel, but none as yet from his father's sheep. For that, it seemed they would have to wait until shearing time in the spring when the wool was sold and next autumn when the lambs were big enough to go to market.

When the payment came in from the hotel on the first of each month, their mother would send Leon and Pete around to all the people they owed money. She had coached them carefully in what to say. "This is a little something on our bill and thank you very much for trusting us," and nothing more. But everyone in town seemed to be in the same boat, because Pete heard them saying the same thing when they paid on their bills. The storekeepers never seemed to mind, because their answer was always the same, too. "Thank you. I understand. These are hard times." It came to be a little game that everyone in town played on the first of every month, and Pete was amused by it.

Pete had begged to be the one to take their payment all the way out to Joe Wabuska's ranch. If Joe were there, he would take the time to stop and talk to Pete as if he were grown up, and Pete would come away from the talk feeling as if he were almost a man.

Then suddenly, going out to Joe Wabuska's ranch became a risk. A stranger came to live at the ranch. When Pete asked Joe about him, he learned that the stranger was a traveler down on his luck, and Joe had given him a job with the business end of the dairy to tide him over.

Pete did not like the stranger, but he could not figure out why. He found out why one day when the stranger met him to take the milk payment. Instead of saying what the other business people in town said, the stranger grumbled, "That's damned little money for a big bill."

On the walk home, Pete debated whether to tell his mother. He told Leon instead, and Leon shrugged it off, saying, "Aw, he's only a stranger. Joe will set him right."

But Leon in all his certainty was to be proved wrong on the Saturday morning when Pete went out onto the front porch to take the mail. Pete did not know why the mailman was embarrassed or what he was talking about when he said, "Now, you tell your mother she shouldn't feel too bad. I got a postcard, too, and so did a lot of other people in this town. But I will bet Joe Wabuska ain't to blame."

When the mailman had gone on his way, Pete sorted through the envelopes until he came to the postcard. The hand-printed words leaped out at him, but it was a long moment before the shaming purpose of the open postcard struck home. The card was addressed to his mother and the message read, "We realize there is a Depression, but we have expenses to pay, too. Unless your bill is paid in full by next week, we must cancel delivery to your house. Eagle Valley Creamery."

Pete paid his last visit to Joe Wabuska's ranch that night. He welcomed the concealing darkness, but he did not go reluctantly. His mind was cold with the memory of the muffled crying that escaped from his mother's locked bedroom, his own taking up of Joe's defense, and the blaming of it all on the stranger, only to have to admit to Leon's crushing argument that Joe Wabuska after all had let himself be talked into breaking the rules.

At the square stone markers that formed the entrance to the ranch, Pete paused only long enough for the two barking dogs to recognize him and fall quiet. Then he crossed the darkened yard that led to the front porch. On the steps, he laid the long white envelope that contained all the money in the house and the note that read, "Please stop our milk now." And on top of that, he laid the boots of soft leather insides and hand-engraved designs outside, that had been worn only once.

14

The snows came early the winter Uncle Joanes came to take care of Pete and his brothers and sisters.

Before the first snow, there had been a week of rain. In any other season, the rain would have been welcome. But rain in winter meant a dreary time of leaden skies, leafless trees stained dark, and back streets turned into a mire of mud. Pete slogged his way to school joylessly. The big hallway, so carefully cared for, was lined with galoshes and rubbers. Its oiled wood surface seemed to be ruined forever with the mud that had been ground into it.

Then one night while Pete slept, the weather turned cold and the rain turned to snow. When he awoke in the morning it was to a white world of snow already piled deep in the streets and on the sidewalks and lying like down coverlets on the roofs so that the houses looked as though they had grown six inches taller in a single night. The bare branches of the trees were bare no longer, but had been transformed to wondrous white cobwebs.

And it kept on snowing, huge dollar-sized flakes drifting lazily but relentlessly down. The heavy clouds kept rolling over the Sierra like an avalanche. There seemed to be no end to them. They went to school and were sent home before classes were done with the electrifying news that Carson was snowbound. The plows were stuck and the main road to Reno was closed. Neither the mail nor supplies nor the *Reno Evening Gazette* could get through. The sidewalks on Main Street were like open tunnels between store fronts and gutters were piled higher than a man's head with shoveled snow.

Pete's mother had unexpectedly been sent to the hospital in Reno, there being none in Carson, for an operation having to do with something called female problems. Luckily she had gone before the big snows came and the road closed.

For the first few days after she left, their father had come to take care of them. Because they saw him so rarely, it had been a treat. He had cooked for them, made the fires, washed the dishes himself, chopped up a mountain of firewood in his spare time, and in the evenings told them how things were going with the sheep in the winter desert range east of Carson City, where the snows were not nearly so deep.

But, because feeding and tending the sheep in winter was too much work for one man, Pete's father decided to spell off Uncle Joanes in the

desert and give him a few days in town. He made the harrowing trip to
the desert hills and brought back Uncle Joanes, then went to stay with
the sheep. It was when his father left that things decidedly took a turn
for the worse.

.

Pete sat transfixed in the pew he shared with his sisters and Uncle
Joanes, refusing to believe what his eyes were telling him. He felt the
red flush rising up on the back of his neck and flooding over his ears
so that they burned like fire. Beside him, he heard Suzette's moan of
incredulity and a smothered giggle from Michelle, who was too young
to recognize the awfulness of what was happening.

It had been bad enough when Mass began and Uncle Joanes insisted
on saying his prayers out loud in a foreign language. Pete had survived
that ordeal by deluding himself that nobody around them could hear.
He had also tried to pretend that Uncle Joanes did not belong to their
family. But that had been futile because everybody knew differently,
so Pete had abandoned the subterfuge and tried to impart through his
aloofness that he did not approve of his uncle. But now, the situation
had gotten so desperate that no delusion of any kind was possible. The
attention of the whole back of the church was fixed on their pew.

Pete knew as well as anyone the proper procedure that people followed when the collection plate with the long handle and the wooden
receptacle was taken around by Mr. Caxton. He had seen it too many
times not to know all the variances.

If a man gave a whole silver dollar, he dropped it into the plate softly
so that he would not be considered either rich or showing off. If a man
gave four bits, he dropped it in naturally so that the clink of the heavy
coin spoke for itself. If a man gave only a quarter, he palmed it in his
hand and dropped it in with a quick flip of his wrist so that it sounded
like four bits. And if a man forgot to bring change, he had a choice of
one of two outs. He could stare straight ahead and ignore the presence
of the collection plate, or he could shrug a little shamefacedly at Mr.
Caxton in a silent message that he had forgotten his change. But he
could not repeat this dodge too often, because Mr. Caxton would regard
him with stony disapproval that conveyed a silent message of its own.
*One lapse of memory is understandable, but don't think you can fool me
twice around.*

Now, Uncle Joanes had gone and shattered all precedent. When Mr.

Caxton thrust the collection plate in front of him, Uncle Joanes had been caught unawares. He had fumbled in his change pocket and come up with nothing. That was bad enough, but at least there was a possibility that the gesture was sincere.

Instead of passing a *you understand* look to Mr. Caxton, however, Uncle Joanes had leaned forward and with difficulty worked a worn black wallet out of his hip pocket. Opening it, he fumbled through its various enclosures until he found a five dollar bill folded into a little square. Setting the wallet between his knees, he painstakingly unfolded the five dollar bill and then, because he was farsighted, held it at arm's length to make sure of its true value. Mr. Caxton waited with pained patience. When Uncle Joanes dropped in the five dollar bill, though, Mr. Caxton's eyes lighted up like a man who had found a gold mine. He nodded his thanks to Uncle Joanes, even managing what went for a smile at the corners of his grim mouth, and proceeded to move on.

Mr. Caxton was brought to a direct halt by Uncle Joanes' horny hand, which reached out like a snake and grasped the collection plate. Relentlessly, he drew it and Mr. Caxton back to the pew. Then, unbelievably, he started to rummage through the plate for his change. He found silver dollars quickly enough, but the smaller change gave him trouble. Drawing out a quarter or a dime or a nickle, he scrutinized each coin at long distance. At one point, he bit his lip as if trying to calculate the amount of his change and the amount of his contribution. When he was finally satisfied, he waved the collection plate and the dignified Mr. Caxton away with a peremptory sweep of his hand. The entire transaction consumed as much time as it usually took for Mr. Caxton to cover the entire church. So much time, in fact, that Father O'Malley glanced back over his shoulder with one of his *What the hell is going on back there* looks.

If the business of the collection plate and all the things that had gone before were not enough to inspire plots of revenge in Pete, what happened after mass was.

Uncle Joanes, who had never had a family, nevertheless had his own ideas about how a family should be run. He imposed a discipline that his infantry sergeant in World War I would have been proud of. There was no more rushing to school in the morning, simply because of the fact that Uncle Joanes routed them out of bed when the stars were still shining. This was to give Pete and his brothers the unheard-of opportunity to make their beds, comb their hair, wash their faces, and submit to inspection. There was no dallying around after school on the sledding hill, because Uncle Joanes's orders were that they come straight home and chop wood and shovel snow from the sidewalks and go after groceries. There was no radio at night because lights were out at eight o'clock, and that left only time enough for homework.

Pete had to admit, though, that Uncle Joanes, for a man, was a good cook. He had had to learn that from his years alone in the mountains and deserts. His one failing was that he loved peas, which Pete did not like in any case and certainly not for every lunch and dinner. And his prejudice against peas grew stronger because of Uncle Joanes's table manners. Instead of using a fork as polite people did, Uncle Joanes ate them with his knife. The knife would disappear into a mound of peas and emerge with a line of them perfectly poised on the blade. When he tipped his head back, they rolled off single file into his mouth with never a miss. Though it was a balancing act that Pete had never seen equaled, he still considered it bad manners.

And it was the question of manners that decided Pete to seek revenge on his Uncle Joanes.

After mass on Sunday morning, it was an unchallenged tradition that he and his brothers and sisters could read the funnies from the *San Francisco Examiner* at breakfast. It was a tradition that their mother had never questioned. Sunday funnies went with Sunday breakfast just as unalterably as Sunday Communion went with Sunday mass.

Not so on the first Sunday morning after the coming of Uncle Joanes. Emerging from the kitchen with a heaping platter of ham and eggs in one hand and a towering platter of butter-soaked toast in the other, he took one look at the table and said, "Get rid of them newspapers."

Pete, who was in the middle of Tarzan, regarded his Uncle Joanes with open mouth. Even Leon, who in their father's absences had assumed a role of authority, had nothing to say for once. From the rest of the family, there was a single anguished cry of protest.

Uncle Joanes turned back to the kitchen with the breakfast platters still in his hands. "All right," he said over his shoulder. "No mind, no breakfast."

"Why?" demanded Pete. "Mama always lets us read the funnies at Sunday breakfast."

Uncle Joanes had disappeared into the kitchen. They heard his voice clearly. "When your mother is here, she can do things her way. When I'm running this house, you do things my way."

"Well, why though?" Pete persisted.

"Because it's bad manners," Uncle Joanes called back.

"He's got a right to talk about manners," Pete mumbled so that their uncle could not hear. "After what *he* did in church this morning."

"He eats peas with a knife," whispered Suzette. "If that isn't bad manners!"

"I'm waiting," Uncle Joanes called out.

Leon was the first to throw aside his part of the funnies. "I don't know about you guys," he said. "But I'm starved."

One by one, they followed his lead. When the last of the funnies were off the table, Uncle Joanes reappeared in the doorway of the kitchen. "Grub's on," he said with smug satisfaction.

It was late afternoon when Pete came back to the house. He had not wanted to leave the sledding hill, but when his joints really began to ache from the wetness of the heavy snow, he had remembered the doctor's warning and decided it was time to go home and dry his clothes.

The sound of the telephone ringing in the dining room carried to his ears while he was sweeping the snow off his boots on the front porch. Though the telephone almost never rang, he paid it no attention, knowing that at least his sisters and certainly Uncle Joanes were at home. When it kept on ringing, it occurred to him that Michelle had probably gone to her friend's house to play and that Suzette was making a solitary visit to church, something she was beginning to do often. That left Uncle Joanes, and why in hell didn't he answer the telephone? Impatiently, Pete leaned the broom against the wall and went into the foyer.

The clump of frantic footsteps and his Uncle Joanes's voice raised to an unnatural key stopped Pete short in the darkened foyer. For an instant, he could not comprehend what was happening. Then he heard his Uncle Joanes's voice again, this time closer and clearer. He was shouting something about a telephone. And comprehension came to Pete. He remembered his father saying that Uncle Joanes just did not get along with mechanical things. He had never even learned to drive, and Pete recalled that he had never seen Uncle Joanes answer the telephone. His panic must have come from that.

Pete saw his revenge. "Serves him right," he thought. "He needs a comeuppance."

When he heard Uncle Joanes's running footsteps enter the living room, Pete ducked into the deep shadow in one corner of the foyer. He waited there, trying to keep quiet, until his Uncle Joanes ran into the room. By now he was screaming, "Telephone! Telephone! Somebody answer the telephone!"

Pete stood in dismay at the aspect of a grown man who could master any horse, who had endured all the hardness of outside life, who had stood up to range wars and gunfights, falling into pieces before his eyes. Pete started to show himself, and then drew back. He could not make his appearance now, emerging from what was so obviously a hiding place. He was trapped by his own vindictiveness.

"I'm sorry, Unc," he whispered aloud when Uncle Joanes had gone back into the dining room. "I'm so sorry, Unc."

After a while, the telephone finally stopped its incessant ringing. Pete tiptoed out through the front porch and hid himself in the lowering dusk and falling snow.

15

When their father brought their mother home from the hospital in Reno, Uncle Joanes wasted no time in going back to the sheep. He went with ill-conceived relief. Everything he had endured confirmed his suspicions about the virtues of married life, Pete was sure. And as for the children, he never even bothered to say goodbye. Pete felt that Uncle Joanes was justified.

Their father stayed around the house only long enough to assure himself that their mother had gotten most of her strength back, and then he, too, was gone.

For some reason Pete could not decipher, their mother relaxed her vigilance over him and his brothers. Pete supposed it had something to do with the discovery that they could actually manage to stay alive without her. It was her first lesson, but not the last she was to learn in time to come. At any rate, freedom—at least for Leon and Pete—included the right to go to Bergen's pool hall in the evenings. There really was nowhere else to go, and their mother knew they were in good hands there under Dutch's scrutiny.

But that all fell into pieces one night, not because of anyone from Carson, but because of the Okies that one saw everywhere these days.

The back of Bergen's pool hall was dim and quiet. Only three cones of light broke the darkness, casting their glow over the two pool tables and the oilcloth-covered card table at the rear of the room. Tobacco smoke lay in heavy wreaths in the cones of light, working its way slowly upwards to be lost in the shadows that reached to the high ceiling.

The voices here were a murmur except for an occasional cry of delight from a pool player who had made a shot beyond his ability, or an exclamation of dismay from a player who had missed an easy one. The men playing solo at the card table did not indulge in either excess, but hunched forward with poker faces and allowed their emotions to show only in the slapping down of their cards.

The old timers who had come in from their shacks and cold rooms in the little hotels sat in a circle around the huge pot-bellied stove, smoking their curved pipes filled with fragrant tobacco, exchanging a word once in a while, but mostly listening to the settling of the coal in the grate and the wind that probed futilely around the edges of buildings and hurled spatters of snow against the window panes.

In his chair in the furthest corner of the room, Pete breathed a sigh of contentment and wished that the Saturday night good-timers at the front would quiet down a little or go on to their next destination at the whorehouses. But he could not really complain about their noise. It was enough that Dutch had fudged his situation a little, since Pete was not in high school yet and therefore, by Dutch's own rules, ineligible to come into the pool hall at night.

Pete's mother had been more than fair about it, too, allowing him to go to the pool hall on weekend nights. Pete guessed, however, that she must have known about Dutch's rules, which included no drinking by anyone until he was eighteen, no bad language from anyone eighteen or eighty, and a shooing off to home of the younger boys promptly at nine o'clock. Woe to the boy whose parents called looking for him after ten o'clock. By Dutch's rules, he would be denied entry to the pool hall for a week, and a second infraction meant running the risk of ostracism for an entire month.

The Saturday night good-timers seemed to be really whooping it up now, but a new note had entered into the usual rowdiness of loud voices and good-natured shoving whenever someone won a throw of the dice cup that meant another round of beers paid for by somebody else. Pete turned his attention from the subdued and comfortable goings on in the back of the pool hall to see what had caused the warning note.

As he suspected, it was the presence of two more strangers to Carson City. They were brothers who called themselves Slim and Shorty. They claimed they came from Texas, but people in town said they were Okies. Pete was not sure what Okie meant other than the fact that they came from Oklahoma. But he had seen the migrant caravans coming through Carson City on their way to California, old jalopies and trucks filled with grown-ups and kids, squawking chickens, dogs and cats, and odds and ends of furniture piled sky high and tied down with a maze of ropes. Pete had regarded them all as if they were creatures from the moon, but he had felt sorry for the gaunt, hollow-eyed women because they looked sad and beaten down. He did not like the men, though, because they looked mean and mad and menacing, as if they bore a grudge against the whole world.

Slim and Shorty were two of that kind. Nobody could figure out why they had decided to settle in Carson City when the rest of the Okies went on to California. But settle they did, working at odd jobs around town and on the ranches and making a general nuisance of themselves.

Somehow, they did not go with Carson City. Perhaps it was because they ambled when they walked or oversrore when they talked. But mostly it was because there was a touch of craziness about them. It was not the kind of craziness that Carson City was used to, but one which carried with it a threat of violence lying too close to the surface.

Slim and Shorty had proved that already. Though Pete had not seen it happen, he had heard of Slim's habit when he was drunk of taking a bite out of his glass and chewing the splinters until blood dripped out of the corners of his mouth. And though Pete had not watched it either, he had heard the stories of how Shorty, when he was finished with a whore, would burn her initials into his arm with the end of his cigarette.

Now Slim and Shorty were breaking the rules again by stomping and shouting at each other at the bar. Because of their strange way of talking, Pete could make little sense out of what they were arguing about. But it seemed to have something to do with the extravagance of one of them in buying a new shirt. Dutch was trying to quiet them down, but he was taking care to keep the bar between them and him, as if he sensed a danger to himself. The other Saturday night good-timers must have sensed the same thing, because they had sidled away to the other end of the bar and some of them had even come into the security of the back of the pool hall.

"Brother or no, I ought to kick hell out of you!" yelled Slim at the top of his voice, and that finally caught the attention of even the solo players at the card table and caused the old-timers around the fire to look around.

"You sidewinder son of a bitch!" Shorty yelled back. "Put up your fuckin' hands!"

This time, Dutch managed to make himself heard. "If you're gonna fight, it's not gonna be in here. Go outside!"

The brothers did not need a second invitation. With Slim in the lead, they peeled off their coats and bulled their way through the front door. Except for Dutch and the old-timers, the rest of the pool hall emptied into the snowy street. Out of fear, Pete held back until Leon and the high school boys made a dash for the door and then he trailed after them, taking care to avoid Dutch's disapproving stare. The last thing he heard as he went through the door was Dutch's disgusted voice, "What's this town coming to, anyway?"

When Pete joined the circle of onlookers, it was to see something he had never seen before, grown-up men actually fighting like kids.

He began to shiver uncontrollably at the sound of powerful men's fists splatting against flesh, but still he could not tear himself away.

At first it was Shorty who was winning. He had sneaked in under Slim's long arms and was battering him with short punches. Then Slim's arms clamped themselves around Shorty in a bear hug. They wrestled for a moment, and then Shorty's hands came together and unexplainably grasped the front of Slim's shirt. There was a ripping sound as Shorty broke free with the tatters of Slim's shirt still in his hands. Slim looked down at his bared chest in dismay. And then he went crazy. One roundhouse swing caught Shorty full in the face, hurling him against the stone front of the pool hall. His mouth open and dripping blood, Shorty slid down the wall and sat in the snow.

The fight should have ended there, but it didn't. Slim took one long step forward, braced his legs and aimed at Shorty's upturned face. Against the background of voices raised in shock and protest, the crunching sound of fist against flesh and bone against stone managed to make itself heard. Shorty's head dangled for a moment as if it had come disconnected, and then his whole body fell sideways. At the place where the back of his head had rested, there was a great gob of blood and brains that worked their way redly down into the white snow.

In the ringing silence, Pete heard the fateful words, "Somebody call the sheriff. This man is dead."

The circle of accusing eyes turned to fix on Slim. But Slim was not paying attention either to them or to the figure of his brother in the snow. Fingering the remnants of his shirt, he said, "Look what that son of a bitch did to my new shirt."

Pete did not see the sheriff come or Slim being arrested or Shorty's body being taken to the funeral parlor. Dutch had made sure of that. Although he was nearly beside himself, he ordered all the boys home in no uncertain terms. They went reluctantly, but they went.

Pete and Leon did not speak until they had left the corner to the main street behind and were making their way along shoveled sidewalks that were filling up again with fresh snow. Pete felt the flakes brushing against his face and heard the measured growling of his boots in the snow, but dimly as if he were walking in a dream. The hushed streets and big trees and solid houses resting warmly under a blanket of snow seemed unreal to him. He was drained and listless and he knew he would have a nightmare when he went to bed.

When the lights of their home came into view, Leon said, "Boy, are they different."

"Who?" said Pete.

"Those people out there," said Leon. "I don't know if I'm going to like it."

Pete figured that Leon meant the world outside of Carson City. It was a new thought. Pete had never considered going out into that world. After tonight, he was not sure he wanted to think about it at all.

16

The lambs lay huddled along the corral fences, nursing their wounds and gathering strength from the gentle sun. In a little while, they would venture to get up and walk on tottering legs in search of their mothers.

Waiting his turn for the washbasin on the log beside the shack, Pete marveled at how quickly they could recover from having their tails cut off, and for the male lambs, from being castrated, too. But it was so, because the lambs that had been docked only yesterday were gamboling in the big corral as if nothing had happened to them. By the day after tomorrow, their father had told them, the whole band would be trailing out into the desert hills to feed on the tender green shoots of new spring growth.

The weekend had started out to be one of disturbing new sensations for Pete and his brothers. Their father had come for them in the darkness, and they had set out into the dawn all jammed together in the cab of the big truck, made warm by the heat that flowed back from the motor. They were not even certain what work they were supposed to do, other than their mother's vague explanation that their father needed them to help *mark* the lambs, and that they would be paid for their work.

They had wound their way on jolting dirt roads into the desert winter range. When they pulled up in front of the dilapidated cabin that was winter headquarters for their father and Uncle Joanes, Pete had stared in wonder at it. Through the long winter when they had been snug and warm in the house in town, he had never thought about where and how his father and Uncle Joanes were living through howling blizzards and frozen nights. He knew now why their faces and hands were burned by cold.

The cabin was the poorest place he had ever seen. Even the shabby Indian shacks on the outskirts of Carson City seemed rich in comparison. There was a wooden stoop instead of a porch, and inside was a single long room smelling of leather and canvas and rancid grease soaked into unpainted old boards that made up ceiling and walls and floor. A blackened cooking stove with an unsteady chimney dominated one end. In the middle was a scarred wooden table with benches, and the other end held two iron bedsteads and a jumble of packbags and packsaddles, sheephooks and branding irons, and a remarkable broom made out of a shredded gunny sack. Imagining that this was how it had been in the poor days when he was too young to remember, Pete fell in love with all of it in an instant.

In the corrals filled with milling sheep and choking dust, Pete and his brothers discovered what their mother meant by marking lambs. There was a bloodstained slab of wood nailed flat onto two corral posts that told the whole story.

They had begun by pushing sheep into a long chute with a narrow swinging gate at the end. Their father stationed himself there, working the gate back and forth so as to shunt the mothers into a big corral and the lambs into a smaller one.

"Now, I will show you how to do it," their father said when the small corral was filled. He reached down with a quick movement and grasped a lamb by his forelegs. Holding the lamb against his chest, he gathered up a foreleg and a hindleg in one hand and the other two legs in his other hand. Then he went to the cutting block where Uncle Joanes was sharpening his long-bladed pocket knife, and set the lamb down on his rump.

The operation was done so quickly that Pete blinked. In one movement, Uncle Joanes folded the lamb's ear and carved out an earnotch. In a second movement, he cut off the end of the lamb's bag and then squeezed out the testicles and pulled them loose with his teeth. Pete heard a moan from one of his brothers and felt his own groin contract. After that, the business of cutting off the tail was nothing.

They had gotten the hang of it in a hurry, and after a day, it seemed to be perfectly natural to be covered with blood and dust. However, this was one adventure that Pete knew he would never be able to talk about with his friends. They would not understand and he would be too ashamed to tell them of the things that went on in a sheepcamp. He reflected wryly that the secret part of his life was beginning to assume the proportions of a burden.

17

What's the matter?" their father said, his thick eyebrows drawing together in a danger sign. "That's pretty good wages for a few hours' work."

Pete and his brothers looked down guiltily at the silver dollar placed on the scarred wooden table in front of each of them. Except for Leon, not one of them had ever had a whole dollar at one time. It was a lot of money, but that was not the problem. When nobody said anything, Pete raised his eyes to his father's and said tremulously, "We didn't mean that, Papa. It's just that it isn't enough." When he saw his father's eyes blaze, Pete added hurriedly, "I mean we want to buy Mama a . . ." He stopped short, seeing the crudely-sewn patches that covered his father's elbows, and finished lamely, "A present for her birthday."

Their father's brow cleared. "Don't worry about it," he said. "She would get mad if you spent a lot of money on her." He considered for a moment and then said, "How much are you figuring on spending?"

Pete swallowed. "Ten dollars."

"Ten dollars!" their father said almost in a shout. He shook his head firmly. "No, not from me. Whether you know it or not, I'm protecting you from big trouble at home."

"How about if we work for it?" said Leon. "There must be some work to do around here."

Their father laughed. "Oh, there's a little work to do around here, all right. But nothing I am going to pay you for out of family money. I don't want your mother mad at me, too."

The brothers regarded each other in silence, and Pete's eyes framed the question, *Well, what're we gonna do?* Each of them saw in his mind's eye the purple dress in the store window with a tag that said $10, and each of them knew that no other dress would do.

A puff of wind from the east came through the open doorway, and their father wrinkled his nose in distaste. None of them knew it then, but it was the wind that was to solve their problem, at a cost dearer than they had expected to pay.

Their father's brow knitted. "Are you sure you want to earn that money?" When they looked at him and nodded, he said, "Have you got strong stomachs?"

Pete had never thought about his stomach before. "I don't know," he said. "I guess so."

"Well, you are going to find out," their father said. "Get some gunny sacks and come with me."

Pete could not imagine where they were going until they had skirted the corrals and struck out toward a clearing in the sagebrush. Then he wished he had not eaten.

Their father did not attempt to conceal his distaste as they stood together regarding the strewn carcasses of sheep that had died in the lambing. In the afternoon heat, the air was suffocating with the stench of rotting flesh.

"I could never bring myself to do it," their father said. "But there's money there even so. Them sheep have got full fleeces, and it's been time enough now for the meat to have gotten eaten up. That wool will pull off easy, and even if it's dead wool, it will bring money in Reno. At least, I will take the sacks in for you and collect your money."

When they were alone, little Mike began to cry. "I'm not going to do it. It's too awful."

"Well, you're the littlest," said Pete, "so you don't have to. Go on back to the cabin."

Pete felt tears in his own throat, as if he had been deeply hurt. *It's not fair,* he thought bitterly. *Why does there have to be money in the world anyway?* Sullenly, he picked up his gunny sack and stepped into the clearing, and the others followed.

It was like descending into a putrid pool of corruption. Pinching his nostrils shut, Pete tried to breathe through his mouth. But when he did that he had no free hand to work, so he gave it up and let the stench come into his lungs. After a while, it was not as bad as it had been in the beginning.

Before he began plucking, Pete warily circled the ewe he had chosen. Her jaws were open and he could see the whitened arch of little bones in her mouth. He reached out and pulled at a tuft of wool. It came away easily, leaving only a bare rib showing. He breathed a sigh of relief, but in restraint, because he still could not afford to breathe easily.

He found himself marveling as he stuffed the wool into his gunny sack. Though it was gray and hard on the surface, the underneath was white and virgin pure. For a reason he could not fathom, this heartened him, and he began to pull great handfuls from the dead ewe, pausing to look at the under whiteness before putting the wool into the sack. In far less time than he had anticipated, the ewe was stripped to a skeleton. He straightened then to see how his brothers were faring. To his surprise, both of them had gone off to sit on a rock.

"What's the matter with you?" Pete challenged them.

"Hell with it," said Leon. "We've got enough. Papa said three bags full, and that's what we've got." He picked up his bag, and with Gene trailing after, started to walk back to the cabin.

"No!" Pete shouted at their retreating figures.

There was a ewe lying apart from the rest to show that she had died more recently than the rest. Her wool probably meant more money than they needed, but it was nevertheless there for the taking. Pete dragged his sack to the rock, glancing disdainfully after his brothers, and picked up the sack little Mike had discarded.

This time, it was not as easy as he had thought it would be. When he pulled at the first tuft of wool, he had to jerk to make it come away. Also, the stench was so overpowering that it set his stomach to cramping and his eyes swimming with sickness. Blindly, he tugged at the wool and thrust it into the sack.

He had stripped the ewe half clean when he first began to notice that his feet were prickling, as if they had gone to sleep. The knowledge of what was happening came to him even before he looked down to see maggots squirming down into the tops of his shoes. With a scream, he fell back on the sand, tearing at the laces of his shoes. When he had gotten them off, he saw that his feet were crawling with maggots, and screamed again.

For an instant, he was paralyzed because he could not bear to touch them with his hands. Then his mind leaped clear and he took rough sand and rubbed them away. When his feet were clean, he stood up and threw his shoes violently into the sagebrush and ran back to the protection of the rock.

Pete raised his head when the shadow fell across him. The tall figure of his father was standing behind him, and the sober gray eyes were taking in the picked skeletons, the ewe lying apart and the half-filled sack near her. His hard hand came unaccustomedly to rest on Pete's shivering shoulders. "When he has to, a man will do a lot of things for money," his father said. "But he's got to know where to stop."

When his father was gone, Pete wiped the tears from his eyes and went calmly into the sagebrush and found his shoes and shook them free of maggots and put them back on. Then he went back to the rock and picked up the full sack of dead wool. He did not even glance back at the half-filled sack lying on the sand beside the ewe.

18

Before the echoes of the fire whistle's last shrill blast died away, Pete knew that it concerned him. It was not a matter of clairvoyance. When one's life in a town made mostly of wood was punctuated by the terrifying sound of a fire whistle, some got so they could sense from the first blast whether it carried a personal message for them. For the others, all activity and all talk came to a standstill while people counted the number of blasts to see if there was a fire in their part of town.

For a moment, Pete had been confused. The signal designating his part of town was two blasts, and the fire whistle had blown three. And then he knew. *Oh, my God,* he thought. *It's the hotel.* Throwing aside the bat, he fled toward Main Street. The firehouse was in one direction and he was in another, and as the sound of the siren from the fire engine grew louder, he knew they would converge at the same point.

When he rounded the corner into Main Street, it was to hear people shouting and see people running or walking, depending upon their age, towards the fire. Dodging from one side of the sidewalk to the other, Pete smelled the burning before he saw the billowing cloud of black smoke climbing into the sky. His heart sank. His sense had been right. It was the hotel.

The big red fire engine had skidded to a stop directly in front, and the volunteer firemen from Curry Engine Company Number Two, with fire helmets on their heads and slickers thrown over working clothes, were scuttling in all directions, dragging out hoses and hooking them to fire hydrants and unlimbering their wicked looking fire axes. The fire chief had clambered pompously down off his high seat and was pushing people across to the V & T depot on the other side of the street.

Pete could see nothing of the hotel because of the thick smoke. Then, red fingers of flame began to make rents in the smoke, and he could see the curtains on fire in the boarders' rooms upstairs. He felt a clutch of fear at the prospect that the boarders were still inside. Then his searching eyes found them standing together in the street.

Because of his high ten-gallon hat, Pete saw Mizoo first. Above his worn Levi's, all he had on were his longjohns. He had lost his shirt and sheepskin coat, but he had not forgotten his big hat and saddle. Mickey McCluskey stood beside him, the ground at his feet littered with shovel and pick and prospecting pan. Pansy Gifford was with them, too. Somehow, he had found the time to put on his baggy old suit and even his necktie. There was a folded newspaper under his arm, and in his lapel, the first pansy of spring. All three of them were taking turns between watching the fire and staring stonily at whiskered old Hallelujah Bob standing apart with his Bible and bottle of booze and a shotgun. Pete edged through the crowd to go stand beside them.

"What happened?" he said, plucking at Mizoo's underwear.

Mizoo looked down. At first, he did not seem to recognize Pete, and then he said, "You growed."

It was Mickey McCluskey who answered Pete's question. With a venomous glance at Hallelujah Bob, he said, "It was him as done it. He got religion and shot a hole through the wall, and that started it."

Pete did not need any further explanation. Just a few months ago, Hallelujah Bob had peppered the walls of his shack outside town for the last time. It had burned down and Hallelujah Bob had very nearly gone up with it.

"Who let him stay here?" said Pete.

"The new proprietors," said Mickey McCluskey. "Though I advised them as to what they was risking."

"Where will you stay now?" said Pete.

"Oh, we'll get along," said Mizoo. "It's just that this old place had gotten to be like home."

Pete turned away. "So long."

"Be seeing you, kid," said Mizoo.

There was a shout of warning from the firemen. As they scurried off to one side, the front wall of The Basque Hotel disengaged itself and toppled forward. Pete drew in his breath. It was like a house whose interior had suddenly been laid bare for the world to see. The high bar and the long dining room table stood where they always had, and beyond that, the kitchen with its massive black cooking stove and pots still hanging on the wall behind it. A rush of unexpected recollections flooded over Pete, and he closed his eyes against the sight.

"There's such a thing as a good fire," a man's voice said beside him. "We need a few more like this one if this town is going to join up with *progress*."

Pete opened his eyes. There was that word again. It was a word heard more and more often now in Carson City. And this man, another stranger who had come to town to form something called a Chamber of Commerce, had said it so many times that the people of Carson City were beginning to say it, too. Pete moved away so that he would not have to listen to him.

"Jeez! I bet this is the most excitement this burg has seen in a long time."

Pete turned his head. There was a boy standing beside him whose clothes revealed him as one more of what people called tourists. He had on a bow tie and a tweed coat with a belt in the back, and knickers to boot. Pete had seen his kind on Main Street and been cowed by their expensive clothes and superior attitude.

The boy was speaking to him now. "What do you fellows do in a town like this?" he said. "Does anything ever happen here?"

Pete could think of nothing that would impress a big-city kid who must have experienced everything. He shook his head. "Not much," he said.

Pete did not stay to see the rest of the little hotel burn down. He made his way through the crowd and across the V & T railroad tracks and over the fence to the lot where they once had played at war. The old barn was still standing, but he guessed it would not be too long before it would burn down mysteriously like the abandoned shanties in Chinatown. Carson City was changing. Everything was changing. And he wondered if he had begun to change, too.

He went inside the barn and looked up at the loft that had been the stronghold of the besieged. When he turned to go, he saw in the pile of rubble on the floor a wooden lathe broken in the middle. He picked it up and remembered instantly the feel of the whittled handle. He laughed aloud in the silence, because he once had imagined it to be a shining sword.